"STAND WITNESS, GIRL, IF YOU HAVE THE STOMACH FOR IT,"

the blond man said. He led the way down a beaten side-trail marked in red.

A hundred yards below the cabin a fifteen-foot ring was laid out, marked by a flat plastic rim of bright yellow and an outer fringe of gravel. The center was flat, finely barbered turf, a perfect disk of green lawn. This was the battle circle, heart of this world's culture.

The black-haired man removed his harness and jacket to expose the physique of a giant. Great sheaths of muscle overlaid shoulders, rib-cage and belly, and his neck and waist were thick. He drew his sword: a gleaming length of tempered steel with a beaten silver hilt. He flexed it in the air a few times and tested it on a nearby sapling. A single swing and the tree fell, cleanly severed at the base.

The other opened his barrow and drew forth a similar weapon from a compartment. Packed beside it were daggers, singlesticks, a club, the metal ball of a morningstar mace and the long quarterstaff. "You master *all* these weapons?" the girl inquired, astonished. He only nodded.

The two men approached the circle and faced each other across it, toes touching the outer rim. "I contest for the name," the blond declared, "by sword, staff, stick, star, knife, and club. Select an alternate, and this is unnecessary."

"I will go nameless first," the dark one replied. "By the sword I claim the name, and if I ever take another weapon it will be only to preserve that name. Take your best instrument; I will match it with my blade."

"For name and weapons, then," the blond said, beginning to show anger. "The victor will possess them all. But, since I wish you no personal harm, I will instead oppose you with the staff."

"Agreed!" It was the other's turn to glower. "The one who is defeated yields the name of these six weapons, nor will he ever lay claim to any of these again!"

The girl listened appalled, hearing the stakes magnify beyond reason, but did not dare protest.

They stepped inside the battle circle and became blurs of motion . . .

THE PLANET STORIES LIBRARY

STRANGE ADVENTURES ON OTHER WORLDS
AVAILABLE EXCLUSIVELY FROM PLANET STORIES!

FOR AUTHOR BIOS AND SYNOPSES,
VISIT PAIZO.COM/PLANETSTORIES

Publisher's Cataloging-In-Publication Data
(Prepared by The Donohue Group, Inc.)

Anthony, Piers.
    Sos the Rope / by Piers Anthony ; [introductory essay] by Robert E. Vardeman ; cover
illustration by Kieran Yanner ; interior illustrations by Scott Purdy.

    p. : ill. ; cm. -- (Planet stories ; #25)

    Originally published: New York : Pyramid Books, c1968.
    May 2010.
    ISBN: 978-1-60125-194-7

1. Regression (Civilization)--Fiction. 2. Social conflict--Fiction. 3. Battles--Fiction. 4.
Science fiction. I. Vardeman, Robert E. II. Yanner, Kieran. III. Purdy, Scott, 1972- III.
Title.

PS3551.N73 S12 2010
813/.54

PLANET stories

COVER ILLUSTRATION BY KIERAN YANNER ◆ INTERIOR ILLUSTRATIONS BY SCOTT PURDY

SOS THE ROPE BY PIERS ANTHONY

PLANET STORIES is published bimonthly by Paizo Publishing, LLC with offices at 7120 185th Ave NE, Ste 120, Redmond, Washington, 98052. Erik Mona, Publisher. Pierce Watters, Senior Editor. James L. Sutter and Christopher Paul Carey, Editors. *Sos the Rope* © 1968 by Piers Anthony. "Honor, Above All" © 2010 by Robert E. Vardeman. Planet Stories and the Planet Stories planet logo are registered trademarks of Paizo Publishing, LLC. Planet Stories #25, *Sos the Rope*, by Piers Anthony. May 2010. PRINTED IN THE UNITED STATES OF AMERICA.

HONOR, ABOVE ALL
by Robert E. Vardeman

The 1960s were chaotic and a time of immense changes. If you didn't experience them firsthand, believe Dennis Hopper in his ad telling you about it. Or if that is too much of a stretch for you, look at the monumental shift in science fiction that took place about the same time the Beatles went from a decent band singing teenage love songs to a group that profoundly altered music to this day. Not only pop culture but everything was changing . . . big time.

From the earliest days, SF predominantly had been a genre of ideas. Action carried plots populated with square-jawed, thewy heroes who never knew fear, moral conflict, or much in the way of internal conflict. Their biggest threats came from outside, usually a scaly green alien with fangs intent on stealing away the buxom blonde heroine, rather than from doubt or moral crisis. You might say they were super men without necessarily being Superman. During the '60s a more literary movement, the so-called New Wave, began introducing characters who lived and breathed and did more than triumph—they also suffered emotionally. The writers increasingly tended to be from English lit backgrounds rather than the hard sciences. Robert Silverberg, Roger Zelazny, Harlan Ellison, Ursula LeGuin, Samuel R. Delaney—all began making a splash with stories of believable people coupled with ideas transcending "simply" saving the world. Along with their explorations of reality and characters' inner conflicts was the sea change occurring in the world outside.

This might be a chicken or the egg problem. Did SF change because society was or did a new group of readers come into the field after *Star Trek*'s unlamented third season wanting something more?

The 1950s saw the rise of the Cold War apocalypse novels. *On the Beach*; *Alas, Babylon*; *Fail Safe*; all nuclear in their destruction, and *Earth Abides*, with a more mysterious plague, dealt with a world plunged back into barbarity, if not outright destruction. The overwhelming sense of horror and loss only echoed what society feared most, possibly with good reason with nuclear saber rattling usually causing a banner headline in the morning newspaper. A swinging Sword of Damocles above our heads was held by the thinnest of threads—and no one could slip out from under it. We were all together in the same small boat that might catastrophically sink at any instant.

The 1960s saw the Cuban Missile Crisis and the escalating Vietnam War but also a mocking of the fear of nuclear annihilation in *Doctor Strangelove* and the growing notion that things could change, through protests and personal belief. Flower children, hippies, the Summer of Love, and a growing awareness of more spiritual pursuits in the world (not to mention drug use) accelerated through the end of the decade. By the time we had landed on the Moon and soundly trounced the Soviets in the space race, society and SF readers were more than willing to embrace the changes offered by the New Wave.

We had gone to the Moon, smashed into a dead end, and had no will to continue to the stars. This was something traditional SF had never in its most pessimistic moment ever considered. "In here" began to matter more than "out there."

Piers Anthony's *Sos the Rope* is a bridge between the old "idea is all" SF model and the most extreme of the "personal angst is all" proponents of the New Wave. The novel combines elements of both and throws in a touch of the nuclear war cautionary saga popular in the 1950s, as well. It is definitely SF, set in a post-nuclear-destruction future with vast areas marked off because of intense radiation, but it follows the hero Sos through a nomadic society using muscle-powered weapons such as swords, knives, and staffs matching what you'd find in a traditional fantasy. Sos is more than Robert Howard's Conan, however, because he is forced to solve conflicts with diplomacy and wit rather than strictly with expertly aimed blade and spilled blood. He is also more than George Stewart's Ish from *Earth Abides* because he is a fighter and never hesitates when he enters the battle circle to settle a dispute.

Therein lies the problem for Sos that he wrestles with throughout the novel. In an affair of honor, he enters the circle and loses not only the right to use any of his weapons but also his name. In a single fight he has become nothing—and is launched on a road that takes him as far from his nomadic culture as possible through his personal change and growth as a human being. Granted the name Sos by the victor, he also discovers friendship in an unexpected place—with the same man who defeated him. From this point, Sos's life becomes far more complex because his new friend and benefactor has plans that entangle him at every turn. He finds a forbidden love, that it is possible to love more than one at a time, and that his talents are greater than a strong arm, and throughout he is constrained by an ironclad sense of honor.

This, as much as anything in *Sos the Rope*, is the central theme. What honor means to Sos and any violation of his sacred word force him down a course of action that today might seem as alien to the new reader as worry about atomic annihilation. Honor, after five decades of moral relativism, means less to us now than expediency, but it is the center of Sos's world. A vow given is one completed. He is willing to abide by the loss of his livelihood and his name, and will not use any weapon because he lost in the battle circle. Indeed, using any weapon at all seems a violation of his code. During the Civil War, a captured soldier might be given his pardon and allowed to freely return home in exchange for a promise not to raise arms against the side capturing him. Such a pledge was kept unques-tioningly. In today's society, it might be kept until out of sight and then violated immediately with no fear of ostracism by friends. If anything, the betrayal of the promise might be greeted with great amusement and approval of the deed.

Sos is willing to die a nameless man rather than go back on his word by so much as picking up a dagger, no matter the provocation.

This "death before dishonor" hearkens back more to Thermopylae than Vietnam. Indeed, Piers Anthony uses classical references in many of his works from this era. In *Sos the Rope*, a prominent feature is a metal mountain known as Helicon. The reference plays on this mythic mountain as the source of the Hippocrene, the spring whose water imparted all poetic inspiration because Mt. Helicon was the home of the Muses. Hesiod wrote in *Theogony*:

> From the Heliconian Muses let us begin to sing,
> who hold the great and holy mount of Helicon . . .

The world of Sos turns more complex than simply dealing with the nomads and the "crazies" who supply them what little instruction they need, along with marking the radioactive parts of the world. But Helicon reveals a new facet of the world to Sos where, again in Hesiod's words, the Muses "dance on soft feet about . . . the altar of the almighty son of Cronos." A man, Sos, must deal with gods who would intrude on his—and humanity's—concerns.

Wrapped up in his honor, and thwarted by its observance, Sos finds himself threatened and manipulated and, eventually, transformed. The collision of cul-tures among nomad, manufacturer, and academic is reflected by Sos, who has touched each segment and has been himself embraced by all three. This is a story far more complex than pitting Morlock against Eloi, as seen through the Time Traveller's eyes. Everyone wants to use Sos as a pawn, but this pawn has ambitions, dreams, and skills. Above all, he has his unshakable code of honor to unerringly guide him through internal soul-searching and external attacks on his values.

The late '60s and early '70s was a watershed of superior SF novels, and Piers Anthony contributed more than his share to this library. *Sos the Rope* was the first of the Battle Circle trilogy, consisting of *Sos* and the later *Var the Stick* and *Neq the Sword*. His 1968 *Omnivore* launched the "Of Man and Mantra" trilogy, which included *Orn* and *oX*, both published in the mid '70s. Certain themes are shared between *Omnivore* and *Sos the Rope*. Both protagonists verge on the superhuman and wander in their own personal wilderness hunting for the meaning of life and death. Honor is key in both characters.

My initial contact with Piers Anthony, other than by reading his novels, came through a fanzine (amateur magazine—a contraction of fan magazine) I pub-lished in the late '60s. It was a heady thing for me when I sent a copy of my mimeographed fanzine to Piers and he responded. For almost a year he both wrote letters of comment and contributed a column, always giving a spirited and cogent presentation of his opinions and definitely enlivening the pages with his trenchant wit. As a tribute to his popularity in the fan press, he was nominated as best fan writer in 1970. His competition was a true giant in the field. He lost to Wilson "Bob" Tucker, a popular fan of almost 40 years at the time with a towering fanzine and convention-going reputation. In addition, Tucker's professional writing career was in full stride with a 1970 Nebula nomination for possibly his best and most famous book, *The Year of the Quiet Sun*.

Piers Anthony's professional work was far from neglected in this era of superior novels. Anthony had two Hugo-nominated books, *Macroscope* and *Chthon*. The latter is a special favorite of mine with its touch of the classical—the word means either a subterranean prison for incorrigibles or a garnet mine. In the context of the book, both are appropriate. Blue garnets still dance in my memory (in our world, garnets come in every color but blue). The book had the unfortunate matching against Roger Zelazny's *Lord of Light*. (Samuel R. Delaney's *Einstein Intersection* and Robert Silverberg's *Thorns* were also contenders. It was a very strong field that year.) *Chthon* also received a Nebula nomination and lost to *Einstein Intersection*.

Macroscope suffered a similar fate in 1970, losing to Ursula K. LeGuin's *The Left Hand of Darkness* in a Hugo field that included Kurt Vonnegut's *Slaughterhouse-Five*.

While being nominated is an honor, there can be no shame in losing to novels that have stood the test of time and are still hailed as among the best the field has to offer. Allow me to say that it would be wrong to leave Piers Anthony's novels off that distinguished roster because he didn't blast off with a Hugo or a Nebula. *Chthon* stands with the best of the field and *Sos the Rope*, hybrid of SF and fantasy that it is, stands at the confluence of Old Wave and New Wave styles, combining the best of ideas and characterization into a novel of scope and meaning.

As his career progressed, Piers Anthony saw the field changing. At times he locked horns with publishers over accounting inaccuracies (and won, sometimes in court). He saw that newer writers needed outlets for their work in nontraditional ways. He was an early investor in Xlibris, a print-on-demand company still in business today. Along with this, he pioneered in e-books and won an Eppie for his staunch support of online writers. He maintains a website where writers can learn of scams and questionable dealings in the publishing world. Perhaps the inflexible honor of Sos is born from the same belief in his creator. More than one grade school teacher has told me *A Spell for Chameleon* not only got their students reading fantasy but reading a wider range of books.

Anthony went on to write the wildly popular and successful Xanth series (of which *A Spell for Chameleon* is the first of 34) and have a string of *New York Times* bestsellers, but the heart (and soul) of his work has its roots in the 1960s. Of those books, *Sos the Rope* is a worthy representative. If you have never read Sos before, you have a treat in a store. If, like me, you are rereading it, the thrill of the days when "sense of wonder" coupled with characters with depth and personal honor meant something will be your companion through the final page.

Robert E. Vardeman
February 2009

ROBERT E. VARDEMAN *is the author of more than fifty science fiction and fantasy novels. In 1972 he was nominated for a Hugo Award for Best Fan Writer, and went on to write the Cenotaph Road series and to co-author the Swords of Raemllyn series with George W. Proctor and The War of Powers series with Victor Milan. He has also written novels set in the* Star Trek, MechWarrior, *and* Magic: The Gathering *universes.*

Sos the Rope

1

THE TWO ITINERANT WARRIORS APPROACHED THE HOSTEL from opposite directions. Both were garbed conventionally; dark pantaloons cinched at waist and knee, loose white jacket reaching to hips and elbows and hanging open at the front, elastic sneakers. Both wore their hair medium: cropped above the eyebrows in front, above the ears on the sides, and above the jacket collar behind, uncombed. Both beards were short and scant.

The man from the east wore a standard straight sword, the plastic scabbard strapped across his broad back. He was young and large, if unhandsome, and his black brows and hair gave him a forbidding air that did not match his nature. He was well-muscled and carried his weight with the assurance of a practicing athlete.

The one from the west was shorter and more slender, but also in fine physical

trim. His blue eyes and fair hair set off a countenance so finely molded that it would have been almost womanish without the beard, but there was nothing effeminate about his manner. He pushed before him a little one-wheeled cart, a barrow-bag, from which several feet of shining metal pole projected.

The dark-haired man arrived before the round building first and waited politely for the other to come up. They surveyed each other briefly before speaking. A young woman emerged, dressed in the attractive one-piece wrap-around of the available. She looked from one visitor to the other, her eyes fixing for a moment upon the handsome golden bracelet clasping the left wrist of each, but kept her silence.

The sworder glanced at her once as she approached, appreciating the length of her glossy midnight tresses and the studied voluptuousness of her figure, then spoke to the man with the cart. "Will you share lodging with me tonight, friend? I seek mastery of other things than men."

"I seek mastery in the circle," the other replied, "but I will share lodging." They smiled and shook hands.

The blond man faced the girl. "I need no woman."

She dropped her eyes, disappointed, but flicked them up immediately to cover the sworder. He responded after an appropriate pause. "Will you try the night with me, then, damsel? I promise no more."

The girl flushed with pleasure. "I will try the night with you, sword, expecting no more."

He grinned and clapped his right hand to the bracelet, twisting it off. "I am Sol the sword, of philosophic bent. Can you cook?" She nodded, and he handed the bracelet to her. "You will cater to my friend also, for the evening meal, and clean his uniform."

The other man interrupted his smile. "Did I mishear your name, sir? *I am Sol.*"

The larger warrior turned slowly, frowning. "I regret you did not. I have held this name since I took up my blade this spring. But perhaps you employ another weapon? There is no need for us to differ."

The girl's eyes went back and forth between them. "Surely your arm is in the staff, warrior," she said anxiously, gesturing at the barrow.

"I am Sol," the man said firmly, "of the staff—and the sword. No one else may bear my name."

The sworder looked disgruntled. "Do you quarrel with me, then? I would have it otherwise."

"I quarrel only with your name. Take another, and there is no strife between us."

"I have earned this name by this blade. I can not give it up."

"Then I must deprive you of it in the circle, sir."

"Please," the girl protested. "Wait until morning. There is a television inside, and a bath, and I will fix a fine repast."

"Would you borrow the bracelet of a man whose name has been questioned?" the sworder inquired gently. "It must be now, pretty plaything. You may serve the winner."

She bit her red lip, chastened, and handed back the bracelet. "Then, will you permit me to stand witness?"

The men exchanged glances and shrugged. "Stand witness, girl, if you have the stomach for it," the blond man said. He led the way down a beaten side-trail marked in red.

A hundred yards below the cabin a fifteen-foot ring was laid out, marked by a flat plastic rim of bright yellow and an outer fringe of gravel. The center was flat, finely barbered turf, a perfect disk of green lawn. This was the battle circle, heart of this world's culture.

The black-haired man removed his harness and jacket to expose the physique of a giant. Great sheaths of muscle overlaid shoulders, rib-cage and belly, and his neck and waist were thick. He drew his sword: a gleaming length of tempered steel with a beaten silver hilt. He flexed it in the air a few times and tested it on a nearby sapling. A single swing and the tree fell, cleanly severed at the base.

The other opened his barrow and drew forth a similar weapon from a compartment. Packed beside it were daggers, singlesticks, a club, the metal ball of a morningstar mace and the long quarter-staff. "You master *all* these weapons?"

the girl inquired, astonished. He only nodded.

The two men approached the circle and faced each other across it, toes touching the outer rim. "I contest for the name," the blond declared, "by sword, staff, stick, star, knife, and club. Select an alternate, and this is unnecessary."

"I will go nameless first," the dark one replied. "By the sword I claim the name, and if I ever take another weapon it will be only to preserve that name. Take your best instrument; I will match it with my blade."

"For name *and* weapons, then," the blond said, beginning to show anger. "The victor will possess them all. But, since I wish you no personal harm, I will instead oppose you with the staff."

"Agreed!" It was the other's turn to glower. "The one who is defeated yields the name of these six weapons, nor will he ever lay claim to any of these again!"

The girl listened appalled, hearing the stakes magnify beyond reason, but did not dare protest.

They stepped inside the battle circle and became blurs of motion. The girl had expected a certain incongruity, since small men usually carried the lighter or sharper weapons while the heavy club and long staff were left to the large men. Both warriors were so skilled, however, that such notions became meaningless. She tried to follow thrust and counter, but soon became hopelessly confused. The figures whirled and struck, ducked and parried, metal blade rebounding from metal staff and, in turn, blocking defensively. Gradually, she made out the course of the fight.

The sword was actually a fairly massive weapon; though hard to stop, it was also slow to change its course, so there was generally time for the opposing party to counter an aggressive swing. The long staff, on the other hand, was more agile than it looked, since both hands exerted force upon it and made for good leverage—but it could deliver a punishing blow only against a properly exposed target. The sword was primarily offensive; the staff, defensive. Again and again the sword whistled savagely at neck or leg or torso, only to be blocked crosswise by some section of the staff.

At first, it had seemed as though the men were out to kill each other; then, it was evident that each expected his aggressive moves to be countered and was not trying for bloody victory so much as tactical initiative. Finally, it appeared to be a deadlock between two extraordinarily talented warriors.

Then the tempo changed. The blond Sol took the offensive, using the swift staff to force his opponent back and off balance by repeated blows at arms, legs and head. The sworder jumped out of the way often, rather than trying to parry the multiple blows with his single instrument; evidently the weight of his weapon was growing as the furious pace continued. Swords were not weapons of endurance. The staffer had conserved his strength and now had the advantage. Soon the tiring sword-arm would slow too much and leave the body vulnerable.

But not quite yet. Even she, an inexperienced observer, could guess that the large man was tiring too quickly for the amount of muscle he possessed. It was a ruse—and the staffer suspected it, too, for the more the motions slowed the more cautious he became. He refused to be lured into any risky commitment.

Then the sworder tried an astonishing stratagem: as the end of the staff drove at his side in a fast horizontal swing, he neither blocked nor retreated. He threw himself to the ground, letting the staff pass over him. Then, rolling on his side, he slashed in a vicious backhand arc aimed at the ankles. The staffer jumped, surprised by this unconventional and dangerous maneuver; but even as his feet rose over the blade and came down again, it was swishing in a reverse arc.

The staffer was unable to leap again quickly enough, since he was just landing. But he was not so easily trapped. He had kept his balance and maintained control over his weapon with marvelous coordination. He jammed the end of the staff into the turf between his feet just as the sword struck. Blood spurted as the blade cut into one calf, but the metal of the staff bore the brunt and saved him from hamstringing or worse. He was wounded and partially crippled, but still able to fight.

The ploy had failed, and it was the end for the sworder. The staff lifted and struck him neatly across the side of the head as he tried to rise, sending him spinning out of the circle. He fell in the gravel, stunned, still gripping his weapon but no longer able to bring it into play. After a moment he realized where he was, gave one groan of dismay, and dropped the sword. He had lost.

Sol, now sole owner of the name, hurled the staff into the ground beside his barrow and stepped over the plastic rim. He gripped the loser's arm and helped him to his feet. "Come—we must eat," he said.

The girl was jolted out of her reverie. "Yes—I will tend your wounds," she said. She led the way back to the cabin, prettier now that she was not trying to impress.

The building was a smooth cylinder, thirty feet in diameter and ten high, the outer wall a sheet of hard plastic seemingly wrapped around it with no more original effort than one might have applied to enclose a package. A transparent cone topped it, punctured at the apex to allow the chimney column to emerge. From a distance it was possible to see through the cone to the shiny machinery beneath it: paraphernalia that caught and tamed the light of the sun and provided regular power for the operation of the interior devices.

There were no windows, and the single door faced south: a rotating trio of glassy panels that admitted them singly without allowing any great flow of air. It was cool inside, and bright; the large central compartment was illuminated by the diffused incandescence of floor and ceiling.

The girl hauled down couch-bunks from the curving inner side of the wall and saw them seated upon the nylon upholstery. She dipped around the rack of assorted weapons, clothing and bracelets to run water in the sink set into the central column. In a moment she brought back a basin of warm water and set about sponging off Sol's bleeding leg and dressing it. She went on to care for the bruise on the loser's head, while the two men talked. There was no rancor between them, now that the controversy had been resolved.

"How did you come by that motion with the sword?" Sol inquired, not appearing to notice the ministrations of the girl though she gave him more than perfunctory attention. "It very nearly vanquished me."

"I am unsatisfied with conventional ways," the nameless one replied as the girl applied astringent medication. "I ask 'Why must this be?' and 'How can it be improved?' and 'Is there meaning in this act?' I study the writings of the ancients, and sometimes I come upon the answers, if I can not work them out for myself."

"I am impressed. I have met no warrior before who could read—and you fought well."

"Not well enough." The tone was flat. "Now I must seek the mountain."

"I am sorry this had to pass," Sol said sincerely.

The nameless one nodded curtly. No more was said for a time. They took turns in the shower compartment, also set in the central column, and dried and changed clothing, indifferent to the presence of the girl.

Bandaged on head and leg, they shared the supper the girl prepared. She had quietly folded down the dining table from the north face and set up stools, while she kept her feet and ferried dishes from range and refrigerator—the last of the fixtures of the column. They did not inquire the source of the spiced white meat or the delicate wine; such things were taken for granted, and even looked down upon, as was the hostel itself.

"What is your objective in life?" the nameless one inquired as they lingered over the ice cream, and the girl washed the dishes.

"I mean to fashion an empire."

"A tribe of your own? I have no doubt you can do it."

"An empire. Many tribes. I am a skilled warrior—better in the circle than any I have seen. Better than the masters of tribes. I will take what my arm brings me—but I have not encountered any I wish to keep, except yourself, and we did not contest your mastery. Had I known how good you were, I would have set different terms."

The other chose to ignore the compliment, but it pleased him. "To build a tribe you need honorable men, proficient in their specialties, who are capable of fighting for you and bringing others into your group. You need young ones, as young as yourself, who will listen to advice and profit from it. To build an empire you need more."

"More? I have not even found young warriors that are worthwhile. Only incompetent amateurs and feeble oldsters."

"I know. I saw few good fighters in the east, and had you found any in the west you would not have traveled alone. I never lost an engagement, before." He was silent a moment, remembering that he was no longer a warrior. To cover up the hurt that grew in him, he spoke again. "Haven't you noticed how old the masters are, and how careful? They will not fight at all unless they believe they can win, and they are shrewd at such judgments. All the best warriors are tied to them."

"Yes," Sol agreed, perturbed. "The good ones will not contend for mastership, only for sport. It makes me angry."

"Why should they? Why should an established master risk the work of a lifetime, while you risk only your service? You must have stature. You must have a tribe to match his; only then will any master meet you in the circle."

"How can I form a decent tribe when no decent men will fight?" Sol demanded, growing heated again. "Do your books answer that?"

"I never sought mastery. But if I were building a tribe, or an empire especially, I would search out promising youths and bind them to myself, even though they were not proficient in the circle yet. Then I would take them to some private place and teach them all I knew about combat, and make them practice against each other and me until they were fully competent. Then I would have a respectable tribe, and I would take it out to meet and conquer established tribes."

"What if the other masters still refused to enter the circle?" Sol was quite interested in this turn of the discussion.

"I would find some way to persuade them. Strategy would be required—the terms would have to appear even, or slightly in favor of the other party. I would show them men that they wanted, and bargain with them until they were ashamed not to meet me."

"I am not good at bargaining," Sol said.

"You could have some bright tribesman bargain for you, just as you would have others to fight for you. The master doesn't have to do everything himself; he delegates the chores to others, while he governs over all."

Sol was thoughtful. "That never occurred to me. Fighters with the weapons and fighters with the mind." He pondered some more. "How long would it take to train such a tribe, once the men were taken?"

"That depends upon how good you are at training, and how good the men are that you have to work with. How well they get along. There are many factors."

"If you were doing it, with the men you have met in your travels."

"A year."

"A year!" Sol was dismayed.

"There is no substitute for careful preparation. A mediocre tribe could perhaps be formed in a few months, but not an organization fit to conquer an empire. That would have to be prepared for every contingency, and that takes time. Time and constant effort and patience."

"I do not have patience."

The girl finished her work and returned to listen. There were no compartments within the cabin, but she had gone around the column to the shower stall and changed. She now wore an alluring gown that accentuated a fine cleavage and a narrow waist.

Sol remained thoughtful, not seeming to notice the girl though she drew her stool close to him. "Where would there be a suitable place for such training, where others would not spy and interfere?"

"In the badlands."

"The badlands! No one goes there!"

"Precisely. No one would come across you there, or suspect what you were doing. Can you think of a better situation?"

"But it is death!" the girl said, forgetting her place.

"Not necessarily. I have learned that the kill-spirits of the Blast are retreating. The old books call it 'radiation,' and it fades in time. The intensity is measured in Roentgen, and it is strongest in the center. It should be possible to tell by the plants and animals whether a given area within the markers has become safe. You would have to be very careful about penetrating too far inside, but near the edge—"

"I would not have you go to the mountain," Sol broke in. "I have need of a man like you."

"Nameless and weaponless?" He laughed bitterly. "Go your way, fashion your empire, Sol of all instruments. I was merely conjecturing."

Sol persisted. "Serve me for a year, and I will give you back a portion of your name. It is your mind I require, for it is better than mine."

"My mind!" But the black-haired one was intrigued. He had spoken of the mountain, but did not really want to die. There were many curious things remaining to be fathomed, many books to be studied, many thoughts to be thought. He had employed his weapon in the circle because it was the established method of manhood, but despite his erstwhile prowess and physique he was a scholar and experimenter at heart.

Sol was watching him, "I offer—Sos."

"Sos—the weaponless," he said, mulling it over. He did not like the sound of it, but it was a reasonable alternative, close to his original name. "What would you want me to do, in return for the name?"

"The training, the camp, the building of empire you described—I want you to do it for me. To be my fighter of the mind. My advisor."

"Sos the advisor." The notion grew on him, and the name sounded better. "The men would not listen to me. I would need complete authority, or it would come to nothing. If they argued, and I with no weapon—"

"Who argues, dies," Sol said with absolute conviction. "By my hand."

"For one year—and I keep the name?"

"Yes."

He thought of the challenge of it, the chance to test his theories in action. "I accept the offer."

They reached across the table and shook hands gravely. "Tomorrow we begin the empire," Sol said.

The girl looked up. "I would come with you," she said.

Sol smiled, not looking at her. "She wants your bracelet again, Sos."

"No." She was troubled, seeing her hints come to nothing. "Not without—"

"Girl," Sol reminded her sternly, "I want no woman. This man fought well; he is stronger than many who still bear weapons, and a scholar, which I am not. You would not be shamed to wear his emblem."

She thrust out her lip. "I would come—myself."

Sol shrugged. "As you wish. You will not be staying in a cabin always, though." He paused, thinking of something. "Sos, my advisor—is this wise?"

Sos studied the woman, now petulant but still lovely. He tried not to be moved by her cleavage. "I do not think so. She is excellently proportioned and a talented cook, but headstrong. She would be a disruptive influence, unattached."

She glared at him. "I want a name, as you do!" she snapped. "An *honorable* name."

Sol crashed his fist against the table so hard the vinyl surface flexed. "You anger me, girl. Do you claim the name I give lacks honor?"

She retreated hastily. "No, man of all weapons. But you do not offer it to *me*."

"Take it, then!" He flung his golden bracelet at her. "But I need no woman."

Baffled but exultant, she picked up the heavy piece and squeezed it together to fit her wrist. Sos looked on, ill at ease.

2

TWO WEEKS LATER THEY STRUCK THE RED MARKERS OF WARNING in the open country to the north. The foliage did not change, but they knew there would be few animals and no men beyond the sinister line of demarcation. Even those who chose to die preferred the mountain, for that was a quick, honorable leavetaking, while the badlands were reputed to bring torture and horror.

Sol stopped, discommoded by the markers. "If it is safe, why are they still here?" he demanded. Sola nodded heartily, unashamed of her fear.

"Because the crazies haven't updated their maps in fifty years," Sos replied. "This area is overdue for resurvey, and one of these months they'll get around to it and set the markers back ten or fifteen miles. I told you radiation isn't a permanent thing; it fades away slowly."

Sol was not convinced, now that commitment was imminent. "You say this 'radiation' is something you can't see or hear or smell or feel, but it kills you just the same? I know you studied the books, but that just doesn't make sense to me."

"Maybe the books are lying," Sola put in, sitting down. The days of forced marching had tightened the muscles of her legs but diminished none of her femaleness. She was a good-looking woman and knew it.

"I've had doubts myself," Sos admitted. "There are many things I don't understand, and many books I've never had the chance to read. One text says that half the men will die when exposed to 450 Roentgen, while mosquitoes can survive over a hundred thousand—but I don't know how much radiation one Roentgen is, or how to spot it. The crazies have boxes that click when they get near radiation; that's how they know."

"One click to a Roent, maybe," she said, simplifying it. "*If* the books are honest."

"I think they are. A lot of it makes no sense at all, at first, but I've never caught them in an error. This radiation—as nearly as I can make it, it was put here by the Blast, and it's like fungus-light. You can't see the fungus glow in the daytime, but you know that light is still there. You can box it in with your hands to shut out the sun, and the green—"

"Fungus-light," Sol said solemnly.

"Just imagine that it is poisonous, that it will make you sick if it touches your skin. At night you can avoid it, but in the day you're in trouble. You can't see it or feel it . . . that's what radiation is, except that it fills up everything where it exists. The ground, the trees, the air."

"Then how do we know it's gone?" Sola demanded. There was an edge to her voice which Sos put down to fear and fatigue. She had gradually lost the air of sweet naïveté she had affected the first evening at the hostel.

"Because it affects the plants and animals, too. They get at the fringe, and everything is dead at the center. As long as they *look* all right, we should be safe. There should be several miles clear of it beyond the markers now. It's a risk—but a worthwhile one, in the circumstances."

"And no cabins?" she asked a little forlornly.

"I doubt it. The crazies don't like radiation any better than we do, so they'd have no reason to build here, until they survey it. We'll have to forage and sleep out."

"We'd better pick up bows and tents, then," Sol said.

They left Sola to watch Sol's barrow while they backtracked three miles to the last hostel. They entered its heat-pump interior comfort and selected two sturdy bows and arrow-packs from its armory. They donned camping gear: light plastic leggings, helmets and traveling packs. Each man placed three swift shots in the standing target near the battle circle, feeling out the instruments, then shouldered them and returned to the trail.

Sola was asleep against a tree, hiking skirt hitched up indecorously. Sos looked away; the sight of her body stirred him in spite of what he knew of her bad temper. He had always taken his women as they came and formed no lasting relationships; this continued proximity to another man's wife acted upon him in a way he did not like.

Sol kicked her. "Is this the way you guard my weapons, woman?"

She jumped up, embarrassed and angry. "It's the same way you take care of *mine!*" she retorted. Then, afraid, she bit her lip.

Sol ignored her. "Let's find a place quickly," he said, glancing at the nearest marker. Sos gave the woman the leggings and helmet he had brought for her;

Sol hadn't thought of it. Sos wondered why they stayed together, when they evidently didn't get along. Could sex mean so much?

He forced his eyes away from her again, afraid to answer that.

They stepped across the line and moved slowly into the badlands. Sos repressed the nervous twinge he felt at the action, knowing that if *he* felt it, the others were stuck much more forcefully. He was supposed to know; he had to prove he was right. Three lives depended on his alertness now.

Even so, the personal problem preoccupied him. Sol had said at the outset that he needed no woman. This had sounded like a courteous deferral to the other man, since no second woman was available. But then he had given the girl his bracelet, signifying their marriage. They had slept together two weeks, yet she now dared to express open dissatisfaction. Sos did not like the look of it.

The leaves and underbrush of the forest and field seemed healthy, but the rustle of wildfire faded out as they penetrated deeper. There were birds and numerous flying insects, but no deer, groundhogs or bear. Sos watched for the traces and found none. They would have trouble locating game for their arrows if this were typical. At least the presence of the birds seemed to indicate that the area was safe, so far; he did not know their tolerance, but assumed that one warm-blooded creature should be able to stand about as much as another. The birds would have to stay put while nesting, and would certainly have developed sickness if they were going to.

The trees gave way to a wide-open field leading down to a meandering stream.

They stopped to drink. Sos hesitated until he saw small fish in the water, quick to flee his descending hand. What fish could thrive in, man could drink.

Two birds shot across the field in a silent dance. Up and around they spun, the large one following the small. It was a hawk running down some kind of sparrow, and the chase was near its end. Obviously exhausted, the small bird barely avoided the outstretched claws and powerful beak. The men watched indifferently.

Suddenly the sparrow fluttered directly at them, as though imploring their protection. The hawk hovered uncertainly, then winged after it.

"Stop it!" Sola cried, moved by the fancied appeal. Surprised, Sol looked at her, held up his hand to block off the hawk.

The predator sheered off, while the sparrow flopped to the ground almost at Sola's feet and hunched there, unable or afraid to rise again. Sos suspected that it was as much afraid of the people as the enemy. The hawk circled at a distance, then made up its mind. It was hungry.

Sol reached inside his barrow so quickly that his hand was a blur and whipped out a singlestick. As the hawk swooped low, intent on the grounded bird, he swung. Sos knew that the predator was out of reach and far too swift for such antics . . . but it gave a single sharp cry as the stick knocked it out of the air and hurled its broken body into the river.

Sos stared. It had been the quickest, most accurate motion with a weapon he had ever seen, yet the man had done it casually, in a fit of pique at a creature who disobeyed his warning. He had thought that it was merely the luck of battle that had given Sol the victory in

the circle, though the man was certainly able. Now he understood that there had been no luck about it; Sol had simply toyed with him until wounded, then finished it off quickly.

The little bird hopped on the ground, fluttered ineffectively. Sola retreated from it, perversely alarmed now that the action was over. Sos donned a gauntlet from his camping pack and reached down carefully to pinion the flapping wings and pick up the frightened creature.

It was not a sparrow after all, but some similar bird. There were flecks of yellow and orange in the brown wings, and the bill was large and blunt. "Must be a mutant," he said. "I've never spotted one like this before."

Sol shrugged, not interested, and fished the body of the hawk out of the water. It would do for meat if they found nothing better.

Sos opened his glove and freed the bird. It lay in his palm, looking at him but too terrified to move. "Take off, stupid," he said, shaking it gently.

Its little claws found his thumb and clenched upon it.

He reached slowly with his bare hand, satisfied that the creature was not vicious, and pulled at a wing to see if it were broken. The feathers spread apart evenly. He checked the other wing, keeping his touch light so that the bird could slip free harmlessly if it decided to fly. Neither was damaged, as far as he could tell. "Take off," he urged it again, flipping his hand in the air.

The bird hung tight, only spreading its wings momentarily to preserve its equilibrium.

"As you wish," he said. He brought the glove to the strap over his shoulder and jostled until the bird transferred its perch to the nylon. "Stupid," he repeated, not unkindly.

They resumed the march. Fields and brush alternated with islands of trees, and as dusk came the shrilling of insects became amplified, always loudest just a little distance away, but never from the ground. They crossed the spoor of no larger animals. At length they camped by the bank of the stream and netted several small fish. Sos struck a fire while Sola cleaned and prepared the flesh. The woman appeared to have a good education; she could do things.

As the night advanced they opened the packs and set up the two nylon-mesh tents. Sos dug a pit downstream for offal while Sol did isometric exercises. Sola gathered a stock of dry branches for the fire, whose blaze seemed to give her comfort.

The bird remained with Sos all this time, moving from his shoulder when he had to get at the pack, but never straying far. It did not eat. "You can't live long that way, stupid," he reminded it affectionately. And that became its name: Stupid.

A white shape rose before him as he returned from the pit, spookily silent. One of the great hawk moths, he decided, and stepped toward it.

Stupid squawked unmelodiously and flew at it. There was a brief struggle in the air—the insect seemed as large as the bird, in this light—then the white collapsed and disappeared into the outsize avian mouth. Sos understood: his bird was a night feeder, at a disadvantage in full daylight. Probably the hawk had surprised it sleeping and run it down while in a befuddled state. All Stupid wanted was a safe place to perch and snooze by day.

In the morning they struck camp and advanced farther into the forbidden area. Still there was no animal life on the ground, mammal, reptile or amphibian, nor, he realized, was there insect life there. Butterflies, bees, flies, winged beetles and the large nocturnal moths abounded—but the ground itself was clean. It was ordinarily the richest of nature's spawning habitats.

Radiation in the earth, lingering longer than that elsewhere? But most insects had a larval stage in ground or water . . . and the plants were unaffected. He squatted to dig into the humus with a stick.

They were there: grubs and earthworms and burrowing beetles, seemingly normal. Life existed *under* the ground and *above* it—but what had happened to the surface denizens?

"Looking for a friend?" Sola inquired acidly. He did not attempt to explain what was bothering him, since he was not sure himself.

In the afternoon they found it: a beautiful open valley, flat where a river had once flooded, and with a line of trees where that river remained. Upstream the valley narrowed into a cleft and waterfall, easy to guard, while downstream the river spread into a reedy swamp that neither foot nor boat could traverse handily. There were green passes through the rounded mountains on either side.

"A hundred men and their families could camp here!" Sol exclaimed. "Two, three hundred!" He had brightened considerably since discovering that the nemesis of the badlands had no teeth.

"It looks good," Sos admitted. "Provided there is no danger we don't know about." And was there?

"No game," Sol said seriously. "But there are fish and birds, and we can send out foraging parties. I have seen fruit trees, too." He had really taken this project to heart, Sos saw, and was alert for everything affecting its success. Yet there was danger in becoming prematurely positive, too.

"Fish and fruit!" Sola muttered, making a face, but she seemed glad that at least they would not be going deeper into the danger zone. Sos was glad, too; he felt the aura of the badlands, and knew that its mystery was more than what could be measured in Roentgens.

Stupid squawked again as the great white shapes of night appeared. There were several in sight on the plain, their color making them appear much larger than they were, and the bird flapped happily after them. Apparently the tremendous moths were its only diet—*his* diet, Sos thought, assigning a suitable sex—and he consumed them indefatigably. Did Stupid store them up in his crop for lean nights?

"Awful sound," Sola remarked, and he realized that she meant Stupid's harsh cry. Sos found no feasible retort. This woman both fascinated and infuriated him—but her opinion hardly made a difference to the bird.

One of the moths fluttered silently under Sol's nose on its way to their fire. Sol made that lightning motion and caught it in his hand, curious about it. Then he cursed and brushed it away as it stung him, and Stupid fetched it in.

"It *stung* you?" Sos inquired. "Let me see that hand." He drew Sol to the fire and studied the puncture.

There was a single red-rimmed spot in the flesh at the base of the thumb, with no other inflammation or swelling. "Probably nothing, just a defensive bite," Sos said. "I'm no doctor. But I don't like it. If I were you, I'd cut it open and suck out any venom there may be, just to be sure. I never heard of a moth with a sting."

"Injure my own right hand?" Sol laughed. "Worry over something else, advisor."

"You won't be fighting for at least a week—time enough for it to heal."

"No." And that was that.

They slept as they had before: the tents pitched side by side, the couple in one, Sos in the other. He lay tense and sleepless, not certain what it was that disturbed him so much. When he finally slept, it was to dream of mighty wings and enormous breasts, both images dead white, and he didn't know which frightened him more.

Sol did not awaken in the morning. He lay in his tent, fully clothed and burning with fever. His eyes were half open but staring, the lids fluttering sporadically. His respiration was fast and shallow, as though his chest were constricted—and it was, for the large muscles of limbs and torso were rigid.

"The kill-spirit has taken him!" Sola cried. "The—radiation."

Sos was checking over the laboring body, impressed by the solidity and power of it even in illness. He had thought the man was coordinated rather than strong, but another reassessment was in order. Sol usually moved so smoothly that the muscle was hardly apparent. But now he was in grave trouble, as some devastating toxin ravaged his system.

"No," he told her. "Radiation would have affected us as well."

"What *is* it then?" she demanded nervously.

"A harmless sting." But the irony was wasted on her. He had dreamed of death-white wings; she hadn't. "Grab his feet. I'm going to try dunking him in the water, to cool him off." He wished he had seen more medical texts, though he hardly understood what had been available. The body of a man generally knew what it was doing, and perhaps there was reason for the fever—to burn off the toxin?—but he was afraid to let it rampage amid the tissues of muscle and brain any longer.

Sola obeyed, and together they dragged the sturdy body to the river's edge. "Get his clothing off," Sos snapped. "He may swing into chills after this, and we'll have to keep him from strangling in wet garments."

She hesitated. "I never—"

"Hurry!" he shouted, startling her into action. "Your husband's life is at stake."

Sos ripped off the tough nylon jacket while Sola loosened the waist cord and worked the pantaloons down. "Oh!" she cried.

He was about to rebuke her again. She had no cause to be sensitive about male exposure at this stage. Then he saw what she was looking at. Suddenly he understood what had been wrong between them.

Injury, birth defect or mutation—he could not be certain. Sol would never be a father. No wonder he sought success in his own lifetime. There would be no sons to follow him.

"He is still a man," Sos said. "Many women will envy his bracelet." But he was embarrassed to remember how similar Sol's own defense of him had been,

after their encounter in the circle. "Tell no one."

"N-no," she said, shuddering. "No one." Two tears flowed down her cheeks. "Never." He knew she was thinking of the fine children she might have had by this expert warrior, matchless in every respect except one.

They wrestled the body into the water, and Sos held the head up. He had hoped the cold shock would have a beneficial effect, but there was no change in the patient. Sol would live or die as the situation determined; there was nothing more they could do except watch.

After a few minutes he rolled Sol back onto the bank. Stupid perched on his head, upset by the commotion. The bird did not like deep water.

Sos took stock. "We'll have to stay here until his condition changes," he said, refraining from discussion of the likely direction of the change. "He has a powerful constitution. Possibly the crisis is over already. We don't dare get stung ourselves by those moths, though— chances are we'd die before the night was out. Best to sleep during the day and stand guard at night. Maybe we can all get into one tent, and let Stupid fly around outside. And gloves—keep them on all night."

"Yes," she said, no longer aggressive or snide.

He knew it was going to be a rough period. They would be terrified prisoners at night, confined in far too small a space and unable to step out for any reason, natural or temperamental, watching for white-winged terror while trying to care for a man who could die at any time.

And it did not help to remember that Sol, though he might regain complete health, could never bed his woman—the provocatively proportioned female Sos would now be jammed against, all night long.

3

L OOK!" SOLA CRIED, POINTING TO THE HILLSIDE ACROSS THE valley.

It was noon, and Sol was no better. They had tried to feed him, but his throat would not swallow and they were afraid water would choke him. Sos kept him in the tent and fenced out of the sun and the boldly prying flies, furious in his uncertainty and inability to do anything more positive. He ignored the girl's silly distraction.

But their problems had only begun. "Sos, look!" she repeated, coming to grab at his arm.

"Get away from me," he growled, but he did look.

A gray carpet was spreading over the hill and sliding grandly toward the plain, as though some cosmic jug were spilling thick oil upon the landscape.

"What is it?" she asked him with the emphasis that was becoming annoying. He reminded himself that at least she no longer disdained his opinions. "The Roents?"

He cupped his eyes in a vain attempt to make out some detail. The stuff was not oil, obviously. "I'm afraid it's what abolished the game in this region." His nameless fears were being amply realized.

He went to Sol's barrow and drew out the two slim singlesticks: light polished rods two feet long and an inch and a half

in diameter, rounded at the ends. They were made of simulated wood and were quite hard. "Take these, Sola. We're going to have to fight it off somehow, and these should come naturally to you."

She accepted the sticks, her eyes fixed on the approaching tide, though she showed no confidence in them as a weapon.

Sos brought out the club: a weapon no longer than the singlestick and fashioned of similar material, but far more hefty. From a comfortable, ribbed handle it bulged into a smooth teardrop eight inches in diameter at the thickest point, with the weight concentrated near the end, and it weighted six pounds. It took a powerful man to handle such an instrument with facility, and when it struck with full effect the impact was as damaging as that of a sledgehammer. The club was clumsy, compared to other weapons—but one solid blow usually sufficed to end the contest, and many men feared it.

He felt uneasy, taking up this thing, both because it was not his weapon and because he was bound by his battle oath never to use it in the circle. But he repressed these sentiments as foolish; he was not taking the club as a weapon and had no intention of entering the circle with it. He required an effective mode of defense against a strange menace, and in that sense the club was no more a weapon of honor than the bow. It was the best thing at hand to beat back whatever approached.

"When it gets here, strike at the edge," he told her.

"Sos! It—it's *alive!*"

"That's what I was afraid of. Small animals, millions of them, ravaging the ground and consuming every flesh-bearing creature upon it. Like army ants."

"Ants!" she said, looking at the sticks in her hands.

"*Like* them—only worse."

The living tide had reached the plateau and was coming across in a monstrous ripple. Already some front-runners were near enough to make out separately. This close, the liquid effect was gone.

"Mice!" she exclaimed, relieved. "Tiny mice!"

"Maybe—because they're among the smallest mammals, and they reproduce fastest. Mammals are the most savage and versatile vertebrates on Earth. My guess is that these are carnivorous, whatever they are."

"*Mice?* But how—"

"Radiation. It affects the babies in some way, makes them mutants. Almost always harmful—but the few good ones survive and take over, stronger than before. The books claim that's how man himself evolved."

"But *mice!*"

The outriders were at their feet. Sos felt inane, holding the club aloft against such enemies. "Shrews, I'm afraid. Insectivores, originally. If the radiation killed off everything but the insects, these would be the first to move in again." He squatted and swept one up in his glove and held it for her to see. She didn't look, but Stupid did, and he wasn't happy. "The smallest but most vicious mammal of all. Two inches long, sharp teeth, deadly nerve poison—though there isn't enough of it in a shrew to kill a human being. This creature will attack anything that lives, and it eats twice its own weight in meat in a day."

Sola was dancing about, trying to avoid the charging midgets. She did not seem to be foolishly afraid of them, as some woman were, but certainly did not want them on her body or under her feet. "Look!" she screamed. "They're—"

He had already seen it. A dozen of the tiny animals were scrambling into the tent, climbing over Sol, sniffing out the best places to bite.

Sos lunged at them, smacking the ground with the club while Sola struck with the sticks, but the horde had arrived in a mass. For every one they killed with clumsy blows a score were charging past, miniature teeth searching. The little bodies of the casualties were quickly torn apart by others and consumed.

The troops were small, but this was full-scale war.

"We can't fight them all!" Sos gasped. "Into the water!"

They opened the tent and hauled Sol out by his arms and splashed into the river. Sos waded to chest height, shaking off the determined tiny monsters. He discovered that his arms were bleeding from multiple scratches inflicted by the shrews. He hoped he was wrong about their poison; he and Sola must already have sustained more than enough bites to knock them out, if the effect were cumulative.

The little bundles of viciousness balked at the waterline, and for a moment he thought the maneuver had been successful. Then the hardier individuals plunged in and began swimming across, beady eyes fixed upon the target. More splashed in after them, until the surface of the river was covered with furry bodies.

"We've got to get away from them!" Sos shouted. "Swim for it!" Stupid had already flown to the opposite shore, and was perched anxiously upon a bush. No mystery any more why the surface of the land was clean!

"But the tents, the supplies—"

She was right. They had to have a tent, or nightfall would leave them exposed to the moths. Sheer numbers would protect the army of shrews, but all larger animals were vulnerable. "I'll go back for them!" he said, hooking his forearm under Sol's chin and striking out sidestroke for the bank. He had thrown aside the club somewhere; it was useless, anyway.

They outdistanced the animals and stumbled onto land. Sola bent down to give the patient what attention she could while Sos plunged back into the water for one of the most unpleasant tasks of his life. He swam across, stroking more strongly now that he had no burden—but at the far side he had to cut through the living layer of carnivores. His face was at their level.

He gulped a breath and ducked under, swimming as far as he could before coming up for air. Then he braced his feet against the bottom and launched himself upward at an angle. He broke water, spraying shrews in every direction, drew his breath through clenched teeth and dived again.

At the shore he lurched out, stepping on squealing, struggling fur, swept up the nearest pack and ripped his standing tent loose from its mooring. If only they had folded them and put the things away . . . but Sol's illness had preempted everything.

The creatures were everywhere, wriggling over and inside the pack and through the folds of the bunched tent. Their pointed hairy snouts nuzzled at his face, the needle teeth seeking purchase, as he clasped the baggage to his chest. He shook the armful, not daring to stop running, but they clung tight, mocking him, and leaped for his eyes the moment he stopped.

He dived clumsily into the water, feeling the living layer he landed upon, and kicked violently with his feet. He could not submerge, this time; the pack had been constructed to float, the tent had trapped a volume of air and both arms were encumbered. Still the tiny devils danced upon the burden and clawed over his lips and nose, finding ready anchorage there. He screwed his eyes shut and continued kicking, hoping he was going in the right direction, while things scrambled through his hair and bit at his ears and tried to crawl inside ear holes and nostrils. He heard Stupid's harsh cry, and knew that the bird had flown to meet him and been routed; at least he could stay clear by flying. Sos kept his teeth clenched, sucking air through them to prevent the attackers from entering there, too.

"Sos! Here!"

Sola was calling him. Blindly grateful, he drove for the sound—and then he was out of the lumpy soup and swimming through clear water. He had outdistanced them again!

The water had infiltrated the pack and tent, nullifying their buoyancy, and he was able to duck his head and open his eyes underwater, while the shrews got picked off by the current.

Her legs were before him, leading the way. He had never seen anything quite so lovely.

Soon he was sprawled upon the bank, and she was brushing things from him and stamping them into the muck. "Come *on!*" she cried into his ear. "They're halfway across!"

No rest, no rest, though he was abominably tired. He strove to his feet and shook himself like a great hairy dog. The scratches on his face stung and the muscles of his arms refused to loosen. Somehow he found Sol's body and picked it up and slung it over his shoulder in the fireman's carry and lumbered up the steep hillside. He was panting, although he was hardly moving.

"Come *on!*" her voice was screaming thinly, over and over. "Come on! Comeoncomeon!" He saw her ahead of him, wearing the pack, the material of the tent jammed crudely inside and dripping onto her wet bottom. Fabulous bottom, he thought, and tried to fix his attention on that instead of the merciless weight upon his shoulders. It didn't work.

The retreat went on forever, a nightmare of exertion and fatigue. His legs pumped meaninglessly, numb stalks, stabbing into the ground but never conquering it. He fell, only to be roused by her pitiless screaming, and stumbled another futile thousand miles and fell again. And again. Furry snouts with glistening, blood-tinted teeth sped toward his eyes, his nostrils, his tongue; warm bodies crunched and squealed in agony under his colossal feet, so many bags of blood and cartilage; and stupendous, bone-white wings swirled like snowflakes wherever he looked.

And it was dark, and he was shivering on the soaking ground, a corpse beside him. He rolled over, wondering why

death had not yet come—and there was a flutter of wings, brown wings flecked with yellow, and Stupid was sitting on his head.

"Bless you!" he whispered, knowing the moths would not get close tonight, and sank out of sight.

4

FLICKERING LIGHT AGAINST HIS EYELIDS WOKE HIM AGAIN. SOL was lying next to him, living after all, and in the erratic glow from an outside fire he could see Sola sitting up, nude.

Then he realized that they were all naked. Sol had had minimal clothing since the dunking in the river, and the others—

"On a line by the fire," she said. "You were shaking so badly I had to get that sopping stuff off you. Mine was wet, too."

"You were right," he said. He had been quick enough to subordinate Sol's modesty to need; the same applied to himself. He wondered how she had gotten the clothing off him; he was certainly too heavy for her to lift. There must have been a real chore, there.

"I think they're dry now," she said. "but the moths—"

He saw the material of the tent enclosing them. She had situated the fire so that it radiated through the light netting in front, heating the interior without flooding it with smoke. She had placed the two men prone, heads near the heat, while she kneeled between their feet at the far end, leaning over so that the sloping nylon did not touch her back. It could hardly be a comfortable position, though from his angle it showed her unsupported bosom off to advantage.

He rebuked himself for his preoccupation with her body at such an inappropriate time. Yet it always came to this; he could not look at her without turning physical, any time. This was the other fear of his erstwhile dream: that he would covet his companion's wife and be led into dishonor. Sola had acted with eminent common sense and dispatch, even courage, and it was an insult to put a sexual meaning on it. She was naked and desirable . . . and wore another man's bracelet.

"Maybe I can fetch the clothing," he said.

"No. The moths are everywhere—much thicker than before. Stupid is gorging himself—but we can't put a hand outside."

"I'll have to stoke up the fire pretty soon." It was cold outside, and his feet could feel it despite the greenhouse effect of the closed tent. He could see her shivering, since she was more distant from the blaze.

"We can lie together," she said. "It will keep us all warm, if you can stand my weight."

Again, it made sense. The tent was not wide enough for three, but if she lay on top of the two men there would be both room and a prism of warmth. Both were in urgent demand. She was being supremely businesslike about it; could he be less?

Her thigh rubbed against his foot, a silken contract as she adjusted her weight. Intimate messages ran up his leg.

"I think his fever is broken," she said. "If we can keep him warm tonight, he may improve tomorrow."

"Maybe the shrew venom counteracted the moth poison," he said, glad to change the subject. "Where are we now? I don't remember getting here."

"Over the pass, the other side of the river. I don't think they can catch us up here. Not tonight. Do they travel at night?"

"I wouldn't think so. Not if they travel by day. They must sleep sometime." He paused. "Straight in from the river? That means we're that much farther into the badlands."

"But you said the radiation is gone."

"I said it is *retreating*. I don't know how far or how fast. We could be in it now."

"I don't feel anything," she said nervously.

"You can't feel it." But it was a pointless discussion. They had no way to escape it, if they were in the fringe zone. "If the plants haven't changed, it must be all right. It kills everything." But insects were a hundred times as tolerant as man, and there were more moths than ever. . . .

The conversation lapsed. He knew what the problem was: though they had agreed on the necessity to conserve heat, and knew what was called for, it was awkward initiating the action. He could not boldly invite her to lay her generous breasts against his naked body, and she could not stretch upon him without some specific pretext. What was intellectually sensible remained socially awkward—the more so because the prospect of such contact excited him, practical as its purpose might be, and he was sure it would show. Perhaps it interested her as well, since they both knew that Sol would never embrace her.

"That was the bravest thing I ever saw," she said. "Going back for the tent like that."

"It had to be done. I don't remember much about it, except your screaming at me 'Come on! Come on!'" He realized that sounded ungracious. "You were right, of course. You kept me going. I didn't know what I was doing."

"I only yelled once."

So it had been in his head, along with the other phantasms. "But you guided me away from the shrews."

"I was afraid of them. You picked up Sol and ran after me. On and on. I don't know how you did it. I thought you were done when you tripped, but you kept getting up again."

"The books call it hysterical strength."

"Yes, you are very strong," she agreed, not understanding him. "Maybe not so quick with your hands as he is, but much stronger."

"Still, you carried the gear," he reminded her. "And you set all this up." He looked about the tent, knowing that she must have carved pegs to replace the ones lost when he uprooted the works amid the shrew invasion, and that she must have hammered them into the ground with a stone. The tent was not mounted evenly, and she had forgotten to dig a drainage trench around it, but the props were firm and the flaps tight. It was proof against the moths, with luck and vigilance, which was what counted, and could probably withstand rough use. The placement of the fire was a stroke of genius. "An excellent job, too. You have a lot more ability than I gave you credit for."

"Thank you," she said, looking down. "It had to be done."

There was silence again. The fire was sinking, and all he could see were the highlights of her face and the rounded upper contours of her breasts, all lovely. It was time to lie down together, but still they held back.

"Sometimes we camped out, when I was with my family," she said. "That's how I knew to pitch the tent on a rise, in case it rained." So she *had* been aware of the necessity for drainage. "We used to sing songs around the fire, my brothers and I, trying to see how late we could stay awake."

"So did we," he said reminiscently. "But I can only remember one song now."

"Sing it for me."

"I can't," he protested, embarrassed. "My notes are all off-key."

"So are mine. What's the song?"

"'Greensleeves.'"

"I don't know it. Sing it."

"I can't sing lying on my side."

"Sit up, then. There's room."

He floundered into an upright posture, facing her across the length of the tent, Sol's still form stretched out diagonally between them. He was glad, now, that it was dark.

"It isn't suitable," he said.

"A folk song?" Her tone made the notion ridiculous.

He took a breath and tried, having run out of objections:

Alas, my love, you do me wrong
To cast me out discourteously
When I have loved you so long
Delighting in your company.

"Why that's beautiful!" she exclaimed. "A love ballad."

"I don't remember the other verses. Just the refrain."

"Go ahead."

Greensleeves was my delight
Greensleeves was all my joy
Greensleeves was my heart of gold
And who but my lady Greensleeves?

"Does a man really love a woman like that?" she inquired meditatively. "I mean, just thinking about her and being delighted in her company?"

"Sometimes. It depends on the man. And the woman, I suppose."

"It must be nice," she said sadly. "Nobody ever loaned me his bracelet, just for company. That kind, I mean. Except—"

He saw her eyes move to Sol, or thought he did, and spoke to cut off the awkward thought. "What do you look for in a man?"

"Leadership, mostly. My father was second-ranked in the tribe, but never the master, and it wasn't much of a tribe. He finally got wounded too bad and retired to the crazies, and I was so ashamed I struck out on my own. I want a name everyone will admire. More than anything else, I want that."

"You may have it already. He is a remarkable warrior, and he wants an empire." He refrained again from reminding her what that name could not provide.

"Yes." She did not sound happy.

"What is your song?"

"'Red River Valley.' I think there was such a place, before the Blast."

"There was. In Texas, I believe."

Without further urging she began singing. Her voice, untrained, was better than his.

Come and sit by my side if you love me
Do not hasten to bid me adieu
But remember the Red River Valley
And the girl who has loved you so true.

"How did you get to be a scholar?" she asked him then, as though retreating from the intimacy of the song.

"The crazies run a school in the east," he explained. "I was always curious about things. I kept asking questions nobody could answer, like what was the cause of the Blast, and finally my folks turned me over to the crazies for service, provided they educated me. So I carried their slops and cleaned their equipment, and they taught me to read and figure."

"It must have been awful."

"It was wonderful. I had a strong back, so the work didn't bother me, and when they saw that I really wanted to learn they put me in school full time. The old books—they contained incredible things. There was a whole history of the world, before the Blast, going back thousands of years. There used to be nations, and empires, much bigger than any of the tribes today, and so many people there wasn't enough food to feed them. They were even building ships to go into space, to the other planets we see in the sky—"

"Oh," she said, uninterested. "Mythology."

He gave it up as a bad job. Almost nobody, apart from the crazies, cared about the old times. To the average person the world began with the Blast, and that was as far as curiosity extended. Two groups existed upon the globe: the warriors and the crazies, and nothing else that mattered. The former were nomad families and tribes, traveling from cabin to cabin and camp to camp, achieving individual status and rearing children. The latter were thinkers and builders who were said to draw their numbers from retired or unsuccessful warriors; they employed great pre-Blast machines to assemble cabins and clear paths through the forests. They distributed the weapons and clothing and other supplies, but did not produce them, they claimed; no one knew where such things came from, or worried particularly about it. People cared only for the immediacies; so long as the system functioned, no one worried about it. Those who involved themselves with studies of the past and similarly useless pursuits were crazy. Hence the "crazies"—men and women very like the nomads, if the truth were known, and not at all demented.

Sos had come to respect them sincerely. The past lay with the crazies—and, he suspected, the future, too. They alone led a productive existence. The present situation was bound to be temporary. Civilization always displaced anarchy, in time, as the histories had clearly shown.

"Why aren't you a—" she cut herself off. The last light from the fire had gone and only her voice betrayed her location. He realized that his sitting posture cut off even more of the heat from her, though she had not complained.

"A crazy?" He had often wondered about that matter himself. Yet the nomad life had its rough appeal and tender moments. It was good to train the body, too, and to trust in warrior honor. The books contained marvels—but so did the present world. He wanted both. "I suppose I find it natural to fight with a man when I choose, and to love a woman the same way. To do what I want, when I want, and be beholden to no one else, only to the power of my right arm in the circle."

But that wasn't true any more. He had been deprived of his rights in the circle, and the woman he would have clasped had given herself to another man. His own foolishness had led him to frustration.

"We'd better sleep," he said gruffly, lying down again.

She waited for him to get settled, then crawled upon him without a word. She placed herself face down upon the backs of the two men. Sos felt her head with its soft hair nestling upon his right shoulder, ticklish tresses brushing down between his arm and body suggestively, though he knew this aspect of her repose was accidental. Women were not always aware of the sexual properties of long hair. Her warm left breast flattened against his back, and her smooth fleshy thigh fell inside his knee. Her belly expanded as she breathed, pressing rhythmically against his buttock.

In the dark he clenched his fist.

5

NEXT TIME, ADVISOR, IF YOU TELL ME TO SMASH MY OWN hand to pulp with the club, I will do it gladly," Sol said, acknowledging his error about the moth sting. His features were pale, but he had recovered. They had dressed him in new trunks from the pack before he woke, and let him guess what he might about the loss of the other clothing. He did not inquire.

Sola had found small green fruit on a wild apple tree, and they made a distasteful meal of it. Sos explained about their flight from the shrews, skimping on certain details, while the woman nodded.

"So we can't use the valley," Sol said, dismissing the rest of it.

"On the contrary—it is a fine training ground."

Sola squinted at him. "With the *shrews*?"

Sos turned seriously to Sol. "Give me twenty good men and a month to work, and I'll have it secure the year around."

Sol shrugged. "All right."

"How are we going to get out of here?" Sola wanted to know.

"The same way we came in. Those shrews are defeated by their appetites. They can't wait around very long in any one place, and there was hardly anything for them to eat in that valley. They must have moved on to fresher pastures already, and soon they'll die off. Their life cycle is short. They probably only swarm every third or fourth generation, though that would still be several times a year."

"Where did they come from?" Sol asked.

"Must have been mutated from the fringe radiation." He began his description of evolution, but Sol yawned. "At any rate they must have been changed in some way to give them the competitive edge, here, and now they are wiping out almost every form of ground life. They'll have to range farther and farther, or starve; they can't go on indefinitely like this."

"And you can keep them clear of the valley?"

"Yes, after preparations."

"Let's move."

The valley was empty again. No trace of the tiny mammals remained, except for the matted grass flattened by their myriad feet and brown earth showing where they had burrowed for fat grubs. They had evidently climbed every stalk in search of food, bearing it down by the weight of numbers and chewing experimentally. Strange scourge!

Sol eyed the waste. "Twenty men?"

"And a month."

They went on.

Sol seemed to gain strength as he marched, little worse for wear. The other two exchanged glances occasionally and shook their heads. The man might make a good show of it, but he had been very near death and had to be feeling the residual effects now.

They set a swift pace, anxious to get out of the badlands before dusk. Travel was much more rapid now that they knew where they were going, and by nightfall they were near the markers. Stupid remained with Sos, perched on his shoulder, and this protection encouraged them to keep moving through the dusk toward the hostel.

There they collapsed for a night and a day, basking in its controlled temperature, safe sleeping and ample food. Sola slept beside her man, no longer complaining. It was as though their experience of the last night in the badlands meant nothing to her—until Sos heard her humming "Greensleeves." Then he knew that no victor stood in this circle yet. She had to make her choice between opposing desires, and when she came to her decision she would either give back Sol's bracelet—or keep it.

Stupid seemed to have no problem adapting to a diet of lesser insects. The white moths were a phenomenon of the badlands only, but the bird elected to stick with the empire even at the sacrifice of his favorite victual.

They traveled again. Two days out they met a single warrior carrying a staff. He was young and fair, like Sol, and seemed to smile perpetually. "I am Sav the Staffer," he said, "in quest of adventure. Who will meet me in the circle?"

"I fight for service," Sol replied. "I am forming a tribe."

"Oh? What is your weapon?"

"The staff, if you prefer."

"You use more than one weapon?"

"All of them."

"Will you take the club against me?"

"Yes."

"I'm very good against the club."

Sol opened his barrow and drew out the club.

Sav eyed him amiably. "But I'm not forming any tribe myself. Don't misunderstand, friend—I'm willing to join yours if you beat me, but I don't want your service if I beat you. Do you have anything else to put up?"

Sol looked at him baffled. He turned to Sos.

"He's thinking of your woman," Sos said, keeping it carefully neutral. "If she will accept his bracelet for a few nights, as forfeit—"

"One night is enough," Sav said. "I like to keep moving." Sol turned to her uncertainly. He had spoken truly when he said he was not a good bargainer. Standard terms were fine, but a variable or three-person arrangement left him hanging.

"If you beat my husband," Sola said to the staffer, "I will accept your bracelet for as many nights as you desire." And Sos understood her nostalgia for attentions other than sexual; this commitment was routine. She paid a penalty for her beauty.

"One night," Sav repeated. "No offense, miss. I never visit the same place twice."

Sos said nothing more. The staffer was disarmingly frank, and whatever Sola was, she was no hypocrite. She went to the best man, wanting his name. If she had to put herself on the line to promote a settlement, she would. There was little room in her philosophy for a loser, as he had learned.

Or did she have such confidence in Sol that she knew she risked nothing?

"Agreed then," Sol said. They trekked as a party to the nearest hostel, several miles down the trail.

Sos had his private doubts as the two men stepped up to the circle. Sol was exceedingly swift, but the club was basically a power tool, not given to clever maneuvering. Even if it didn't show in ordinary travel, Sol's recent illness was bound to have its effect upon his strength and endurance in battle. The staff was a defensive weapon, well suited to a prolonged encounter, while the club rapidly sapped the strength of the wielder. Sol had committed himself foolishly and given himself the very worst chance.

Yet what did it matter to him? If Sol won, the tribe had its first real member. If he lost, Sola would take another bracelet and become Sava, and likely be free shortly thereafter. Sos could not be certain which alternative would benefit him personally, if either did. Best to let the circle decide.

No! He had agreed to serve Sol, in exchange for a name. He should have seen to it that Sol's chances were good. As it was, he had already let the man down, when he should have been alert. Now he could only hope that his lapse did not cost Sol the victory.

The two men entered the ring, and the contest began immediately. There were no manners in the battle circle, only victory and defeat.

Sav sparred, expecting a fierce attack. It did not come. The staff was about six and a half feet long and the same diameter as a singlestick, with square-cut ends; it flexed slightly when put under strain, but otherwise was nothing more or less than a rigid pole. It was one of the easiest weapons to use, though it seldom led to a quick decision. It readily blocked any other instrument, but was as easily blocked itself.

Sol feinted four times with the heavy club, watching the defensive posture of his opponent, then shrugged and lashed out with a backhand blow to the chest that neatly bypassed the horizontal shaft.

Sav looked surprised, fighting for the wind and steam that had been knocked out of him. Sol placed his club gently against the staff and pushed. The man fell backwards out of the circle.

Sos was amazed. It had looked so simple, as though a lucky blow, but he knew it was not. Sol had expertly tested his opponent's reflexes, then struck with such quick precision that no parry had been feasible. It was a remarkable feat with the crude club—and no accident. Sol, nothing special outside the circle,

was a tactical genius within it. A man had been added to the group, efficiently and virtually uninjured.

It appeared Sol needed no advice on terms of combat.

Sav took it philosophically. "I looked pretty foolish, didn't I, after all my talk," he said, and that was all. He didn't mope and he made no further overtures to Sola.

The law of averages Sos had read about indicated that it would be a couple of weeks before they encountered any really able warrior. That afternoon, notwithstanding, they met two men with swords, Tor and Tyl. The first was swarthy and greatbearded, the second slim and clean-shaven. Sworders often shaved, as did daggers; it was an unofficial mark of their specialty, since it subtly hinted their skill with the blade. Sos had tried to shave with his sword once and had sliced his face severely; after that he stuck to the shears and did not try for closeness. There were electric razors in the cabins, though few men condescended to use them. He had never understood why it should be considered degrading to use the crazies' razors, while all right to eat their food, but that was the way convention had it.

Both sworders were married, and Tor had a little girl. They were friends, but it turned out that Tyl was the master of the group of two. Both agreed to fight, Tor first, with the stipulation that what he won belonged to Tyl. That was the way of a tribe of any size.

Against Tor, Sol took a matching sword. These were straight, flat, slashing instruments twenty inches long, pointed but seldom used for stabbing. Sword contests were usually dramatic and swift.

Unfortunately, wounds were frequent, too, and deaths not uncommon. That was why Sol had taken the staff against Sos, weeks ago; he had really been sure of his skill and had not wanted to risk injuring his opponent seriously.

"His wife and daughter are watching," Sola murmured beside him. "Why does he match weapons?"

Sos understood her question to mean Tora and Tori as spectators and Sol's matching sword to sword. "Because Tyl is also watching," he told her.

Tor was powerful and launched a vigorous attack, while Sol merely fended him off. Then Sol took his turn on the offense, hardly seeming to make an effort yet pressing the other man closely. After that there was a pause in the circle as neither attacked.

"Yield," Tyl said to his man.

Tor stepped out and it was over, bloodlessly after all. The little girl gaped, not understanding, and Sola shared this confusion, but Sos had learned two important things. First, he had seen that Tor was an expert sworder who might very well have defeated Sos himself in combat. Second, he knew Tyl was even better. This was a rare pair to come upon so casually, after going so long without meeting anyone of caliber—except that that was the way the averages worked.

Sola had thought that sword against sword meant inevitable bloodshed, but in this situation the truth was opposite. Tor had felt out Sol, and been felt out in turn, neither really trying for a crippling blow. Tyl had watched, not his own man whose capabilities he knew, but Sol, and made his judgment. He had seen what Sos had seen: that Sol possessed a clear advantage in technique and would almost certainly prevail in the end. Tyl had been sensible: he had yielded his man before the end came, accepting the odds. Perhaps the little girl was disappointed, thinking her father invulnerable—but her education in this respect would have been rude indeed.

"I see," Sola said, keeping her voice low. "But suppose they had been just about even?'

Sos didn't bother to answer.

As it was, Sol had won painlessly again, and added a good man to his roster. Only by employing a weapon Tyl knew well could he have made his point so clearly.

Sos had maintained a wait-and-see attitude on Sol's plans for empire, knowing how much more than speed and versatility in the circle was required. His doubts were rapidly evaporating. If Sol could perform like this in the time of his weakness, there seemed to be no practical limit to his capabilities as he regained strength. He had now demonstrated superlative proficiency with staff, club and sword, and had never been close to defeat. There seemed to be no barrier to continued additions to his tribe.

Tyl stood up and presented a surprise of his own: he set aside his sword and brought out a pair of singlesticks. He was a man of two weapons and had decided not to tackle Sol with the one just demonstrated.

Sol only smiled and drew out his own sticks.

The fight was swift and decisive, as Sos had expected after witnessing the skill of Sol's wrist. The four sticks flashed and spun, striking, thrusting and blocking, acting both as dull swords and light staffs. This was a special art, for two implements had to be controlled and parried simultaneously, and excellent coordination was required. It was hardly possible for those outside the circle to tell which man had the advantage—until one stick flew out of the circle, and Tyl backed out, half disarmed and defeated. There was blood on the knuckles of his left hand where the skin had been broken by Sol's connection.

Yet bruises were appearing upon Sol's body, too, and blood dripped from a tear over his eye. The battle had not been one-sided.

Three men now belonged to his group, and two were not beginners.

Two weeks later Sos had his twenty men. He led them back toward the badlands, while Sol went on alone except for Sola.

6

"PITCH YOUR TENTS WELL UP ON THE HILLSIDE, TWO MEN OR one family to a unit, with a spare pack stacked across the river," Sos directed the group when they arrived in the valley. "Two men will walk guard day and night around the perimeter; the rest will work by day and be confined to their tents by night, without exception. The night guards will be entirely covered with mesh at all times and will scrupulously avoid any contact with the flying white moths. There will be a four-man hunting party and a similar carrying party each day. The rest will dig our trench."

"Why?" one man demanded. "What's the point of all this foolishness?" It was Nar, a blustering dagger who did not accept orders readily.

Sos told them why.

"You expect us to believe such fantastic stories by a man without a weapon?" Nar shouted indignantly. "A man who raises birds instead of fighting?"

Sos held his temper. He had known that something like this would come up. There was always some boor who thought that honor and courtesy did not extend beyond the circle. "You will stand guard tonight. If you don't choose to believe me, open your face and arms to the moths." He made the other assignments, and the men got busy setting up the camp.

Tyl approached him. "If there is trouble with the men . . ." he murmured.

Sos understood him. "Thanks," he said gruffly.

There was time that afternoon to mark off the trench he had in mind. Sos took a crew of men and laid out light cord, tying it to pegs hammered into the ground at suitable intervals. In this fashion, they marked off a wide semicircle enclosing the packs stored beside the river with a radius of about a quarter mile.

They ate from stored rations well before dusk, and Sos made a personal inspection of all tents, insisting that any defects be corrected immediately. The object was to have each unit tight: no space open large enough for a moth to crawl through. There were grumbles, but it was done. As night filled the valley, all but the two marching guards retired to their tents, there to stay sealed in until daylight.

Sos turned in, satisfied. It was a good beginning. He wondered where the moths hid during the day, where neither sun nor shrew could find them.

Sav, who shared his tent, was not so optimistic. "There's going to be trouble in Red River Valley," he remarked in his forthright manner.

"Red River Valley?"

"From that song you hum all the time. I know 'em all. 'Won't you think of the valley you're leaving, Oh, how lonely and sad it will be; Oh, think of the fond heart you're breaking, and the grief—'"

"All *right*!" Sos exclaimed, embarrassed.

"Well, they aren't going to like digging and carrying," Sav continued, his usually amiable face serious. "And the kids'll be hard to keep in at night. They don't pay much attention to regulations, you know. If any of them get stung and die—"

"Their parents will blame *me*. I know." Discipline was mandatory. It would be necessary to make a convincing demonstration before things got out of hand.

The opportunity came sooner than he liked. In the morning Nar was discovered in his tent. He had not been stung by the moths. He was sound asleep.

Sos called an immediate assembly. He pointed out three men at random. "You are official witnesses. Take note of everything you see this morning and remember it." They nodded, perplexed.

"Take away the children," he said next. Now the mothers were upset, knowing that they were about to miss something important; but in a few minutes only the men and about half the women remained.

He summoned Nar. "You are accused of dereliction in the performance of your duty. You were assigned to mount guard, but you slept in the tent instead. Have you any defense to make?"

Nar was vexed at being caught but decided to bluster it out. "What are you going to do about it, bird-man?"

This was the awkward point. Sos could not take up his sword and remain true to his oath, though he had no doubt of his ability to handle this man in the circle. He could not afford to wait the weeks until Sol would show up again. He had to take action now.

"Children might have died through your neglect," he said. "A tent might have been torn unnoticed, or the shrews might have come after all by night. Until we have security from these dangers, I can not allow one man's laziness to endanger the group."

"*What* danger? How come none of us have seen this terrible horde of itty-bitty critters?" Nar exclaimed, laughing. There were a few smiles around the group. Sos saw that Sav was not smiling; he had predicted this.

"I'm granting you a trial, however," Sos said evenly. "By combat."

Nar drew his two daggers, still laughing. "I'm gonna carve me a big bird!"

"Take care of the matter, Tyl," Sos said, turning away. He forced his muscles to relax so that he would not show his tension, knowing that he would be branded a coward.

Tyl stepped forward, drawing his sword. "Make a circle," he said.

"Now just a minute!" Nar protested, alarmed. "It's him I got the fight with. Bird-brain, there."

Stupid perched on Sos's shoulder, and for once he wished the bird's loyalty lay elsewhere.

"You owe service to Sol," Tyl said, "and the forfeit is your life, as it is for all of us. He appointed Sos leader of this party, and Sos has appointed me to settle matters of discipline."

"All *right*!" Nar shouted, brazen through his fear. "Try one of *these* in your gut!"

Sos continued to face away as the sounds of battle commenced. He was not proud of himself or of what he had to do, but he had seen no alternative. If this action served to prevent recurrences, it was worth it. It had to be.

There was a scream and a gurgle, followed by the thud of a body hitting the ground. Tyl came up to stand beside him, wiping the bright life blood from his sword. "He was found guilty," he said gently.

Why, then, was it Sos who felt guilty?

In a week the trench was complete, and the crews were working on the ramp just inside it. Sos insisted that the bottom of the trench be level and that the water be diverted to flow through it steadily. "Little dribble like that won't stop the beasties," Sav remarked dubiously. "Anyhow, didn't you say they could swim?"

"Right." Sos went on to supervise the installation of mounted fire-strikers, set in the inner edge of the trench and spaced every hundred yards.

Meanwhile the bearers were hauling drums of alcohol from all cabins in range—but not for drinking. They were stored at intervals along the ramp.

Another week passed, and still the shrews did not come. A row of battle circles was set up, and a huge central tent fashioned of sewn family-tent sheets—but the group continued to camp at night in the tight little tents across the river. The hunting parties reported that game was moving into the area: deer and wild goats, followed by wolves and large cats and a few fierce pigs, as well as more numerous rodents. There was fresh meat for all.

Tyl went on enforcing discipline, usually with the sticks; one execution, though of doubtful validity, had been enough. But the seeming pointlessness of the labor made the men surly; they were accustomed to honorable fighting, not menial construction, and they did not like taking orders from a coward who bore no weapon.

"It would be better if you did it yourself," Sav said, commenting on one of Tyl's measures. "It needs to be done—we all know that—but when he does it it makes *him* the leader. No one respects you—and that bird doesn't help much, either."

Sav was such a harmless, easygoing sort that it was impossible to take offense at what he said. It was true: Sos was accomplishing his purpose at the expense of his reputation, which had not been good to begin with. None of these people knew the circumstances of his deprivation of weapons or his bond to Sol, and he did not care to publicize it.

Tyl was the *de facto* leader of the valley group—and if Sol did not return, Tyl would surely take over. He had had aspirations for a tribe of his own, and he was a highly skilled warrior. Like Sol, he had spurned inept opponents, and so had accumulated only one tribesman in his travels; but also like Sol, he was quick enough to appreciate what could be done with ordinary men once the way was shown. Was he being genuinely helpful—or was he biding his time while he consolidated the group around himself?

Sos could not carry a weapon. He was dependent upon Tyl's good will and his own intellectual abilities. He had a year of service to give, and he meant to complete it honorably. After that—

At night it was Sola's face he saw, and Sola's body he felt touching his, her hair upon his shoulder. Here, too, he would never prevail without a weapon. The truth was that he was as dangerous to Sol's ambitions as was Tyl, because he wanted what only complete leadership would bring. Sola would not accept the bracelet of the second warrior of the tribe, or the third or fourth. She had been candid about that.

Yet even if he carried a weapon, he could not defeat Sol in the circle, or even Tyl. It would be fatally unrealistic ever to assume otherwise. To that extent his disarmed state was his protection.

Finally the shrews struck. They boiled over the hillside in mid-afternoon and steamed toward the camp defenses. He was almost glad to see them; at least this would vindicate his elaborate precautions. They had been gone a long time, as the resurgence of game proved; it would have destroyed his program, paradoxically, if they had not come at all.

"Dump the barrels!" he shouted, and the men assigned to this task and drilled for it repetitively knocked open the containers of alcohol and began pouring them carefully into that shallow moat.

"Women and children to the tents!" Protesting shrilly, now that the excitement had come, the families forded the river and mounted the hillside.

"Stand by with weapons!" And all those not otherwise occupied took up the defensive formation, somewhat shamefaced as they saw the size of their adversaries. There were fifteen men and several of the older boys present; the hunting party happened to be out.

The barrel-dumpers finished their job, not without regretful glances at the good intoxicant going to waste, and stood by the extended wooden handles of the fire-strikers. Sos held off, hoping that the hunters would appear, but there was no sign of them.

The shrews surged up to the moat and milled about, mistrusting the smell of it. Then, as before, the bolder ones plunged in, and the mass crossing commenced. Sos wondered whether the animals could become intoxicated in the same fashion as men.

"Fire!" he yelled. The assigned drummer beat a slow, regular cadence, and in absolute unison the men struck the igniters and leaped back. This had been one of the really sore spots of the training: grown men dancing to a musical rhythm.

A sheet of flame shot up from the moat, and the stench and smoke of improperly combusted alcohol filled the air. They were fenced in by a rising semicircle of fire. Watching it, the "dancers" shielded their eyes and gaped; now they understood what could have happened to the late man.

Sos had worked this out carefully. He knew from his readings that alcohol in its various forms would float on water and, if ignited, would burn more readily there than on land, where dirt or wood would absorb it. The layer of water in the moat offered a perfect surface for it, and the current would carry it along the entire perimeter. He was glad to have the proof; even he had had his doubts, since common sense encouraged him to believe that water quenched all fires. Why hadn't he thought to spill a few drops of the stuff into a basin of water and experiment?

Some animals had gotten through. The men were busy already beating the ground with sticks and clubs, trying to flatten the savage but elusive creatures. Several warriors cursed as they were bitten. There was no longer any reason to disparage the ferocity of the tiny enemies.

The burning vapors sank; the alcohol volatized too rapidly to last long. At Sos's signal the men rolled up more barrels from the big central tent. Here they stopped—they could not dump more alcohol until the blaze died entirely, or they would be trapped in the midst of the rising fire and possibly blown apart by ignition of the barrels themselves. This was a problem Sos had not anticipated; the main conflagration had subsided, but individual flames would remain for some time at the canal banks where fuel had seeped into the ground.

Tor the sworder came up, his black beard singed. "The upper end is clear," he gasped. "If you dump there—"

Sos cursed himself for not thinking of that before. The current had swept the upriver section of the moat clean, and the shrews were already swarming across to consume their roasted vanguard and climb the breastwork. Alcohol could be dumped there a barrel at a time, and the current would feed it through the entire retrenchment at a reduced rate and enable them to maintain a controlled fire. "Take care of it!" he told Tor, and the man ran off, shouting to those nearby for help.

Everyone was occupied, stamping and striking at the endless supply of miniature appetites. The swarm beyond the moat reminded Sos again of a division of invading ants, except that the mammals lacked the organization of the insects. The flames came up again as Tor put his plan into operation, but somehow the numbers of the enemy did not seem to diminish. Where were they coming from?

He found out. The shrews were swimming out into the river and recurving to land within the protected semicircle! Most of them did not make it, since there was no coherent organization to their advance; they either got caught in the fringe fire or went straight across to land on the opposite shore. Many drowned in the center current, and more died fighting in the water for the corpses, but the supply was such that even five or ten per cent drifting back into the open area behind the parapet was enough to overrun the area.

Would alcohol dumped directly into the river stop them? Sos ruled it out quickly. There was not enough left, and if it did *not* do the job the entire human party could be trapped by the lingering fires of its own defense, while the animals inundated the base.

He decided to cut his losses. The shrews had won this battle. "Evacuate!"

The men, once contemptuous of the enemy, had had enough. Shrews decorated arms and legs and wriggled in pantaloons and carpeted the ground, teeth everywhere. Warriors dived into the river and swam for safety, ducking under the surface whenever they could, in full retreat. Sos made a quick check to see that no wounded remained, and followed.

It was now late afternoon. Was there time to move the tents back before nightfall? Or would the shrews stop before reaching the present encampment? He had to decide in a hurry.

He could not take the risk. "Pick up tents and move back as far as you can before dusk," he shouted. "Single men may camp here and stand guard." He had stored the duplicate packs within the enclosure in case the shrews attacked from the unexpected side of the river, and those reserves were now inaccessible. Another error in judgment—yet until he was sure of the route and timing of the hordes, such losses would occur.

The shrews did not ascend the hill that night. This species, at least, was a daytime marauder. Perhaps the moths saw to that. In the morning the main body, gorged on its casualties and still numberless, crossed the river and marched downstream. Only a few hardy climbers on the outskirts reached the tents.

Sos looked about. He could not assume that this was a safe location, and it was certainly not as convenient as the valley plain. There was no more wildlife here than below. It might merely mean that the shrews' route was random; obviously they could overrun the hill if they chose to. Most likely they followed the general contours of the land, ascending where there was smoother going, and came *down* at this point when they came this way.

At least he had learned one thing: the shrews traveled only in the group, and thus were governed by group dynamics. He strained to remember the commentary in a complex text on the subject, that he had not suspected would ever have meaningful application to his life. Groups were shaped by leaders and reflected the personalities and drives of those leaders; divert the key individuals, and you diverted the pack. He would have to think about that, and apply it to this situation.

It would also be wise to spy on the continuing progress of the horde and learn for certain what finally happened to it. And to trace its origin—there might be a restricted breeding ground that could be put to the fire before the next swarm became a menace. He had been preoccupied with defense, and he saw now that that wouldn't work.

By noon the enemy was gone, and the men were able to recover their campsite. It was a ruin; even nylon was marked by the bite of myriad teeth and fouled by layers of dung.

A committee plunged eagerly into the problem of shrew tracing and diversion, while women and children moved into the main semicircle to clean up and pitch new tents. It seemed as safe a place as any, since the following horde would starve if it followed the identical route of this one. The next shrew foray was more likely to come down the opposite bank. Besides, there was a great deal of laundry to do in the river.

The bones and gear of the missing hunting party were discovered three miles upriver. Suddenly everyone appreciated the menace properly, and no more grumbles about the work were heard. Sos, too, was treated with somewhat more respect than hitherto. He had proved his point.

7

SOL ARRIVED TWO WEEKS LATER WITH ANOTHER GROUP OF FIFTY men. He now had a fair-sized tribe of sixty-five warriors, though the majority of these were inexperienced and untrained youths. The best men were still tied up in established tribes, as Sos had pointed out in their discussion—but that situation would change in due course.

Sos trotted out the witnesses to the execution of Nar and had them describe to Sol what they had observed. There were only two; the third had been a hunter on the day of warfare. Sos was not certain how the master of the tribe would take it, since his management of the valley group had cost five men. That was a full quarter of the complement put in his charge.

"There were two guards?" Sol inquired.

The witnesses nodded. "Always."

"And the other that night did not report that the first was sleeping?"

Sos clapped his palm to his forehead. For a man who fancied his brain, he had blundered ridiculously. Two had been guilty, not one.

In the end Tyl had another job with the sticks, while Sos and Sol retired for a private consultation. Sos described in detail the events of the past five weeks, and this time Sol's attention never wandered. He had little patience with history or biology, but the practical matters of empire building were of prime interest to him. Sos wondered whether the man had also had some intervening experience with the problems of discipline. It seemed likely.

"And you can form these new men into a group that will conquer other tribes?" Sol inquired, wanting the reassurance.

"I think I can, in six months, now that we have plenty of men and good grounds. Provided they will obey me implicitly."

"They obey Tyl."

Sos looked at him, disturbed. He had expected to have Sol's direct backing for this longer haul. "Aren't you going to stay here?"

"I go out tomorrow to recruit more men. I leave their training to you."

"But sixty-five warriors! There is bound to be trouble."

"With Tyl, you mean? Does he want to be the leader?" Sol was perceptive enough, where his empire was concerned.

"He has never said so, and he has stood by me steadily," Sos admitted, wanting to be fair. "But he would not be human if he did not think in such terms."

"What is your advice?"

Now it was in his own lap again. At times Sol's faith in him was awkward. He could not demand that the master stay with his tribe; Sol evidently liked recruiting. He could ask him to take Tyl with him—but that would only require his replacement as disciplinary leader, and the next man would present much the same problem. "I have no evidence that Tyl lacks honor," he said. "I think it would be best to give him good reason to stay with your tribe. That is, show him that he stands to profit more by remaining with you than by striking out on his own, with or without any of the present group."

"He stands to profit the loss of his *head* if he moves against me!"

"Still—you could designate him first warrior, in your absence, and put him in charge of his own group. Give him a title to sport, so to speak."

"But I want you to train my men."

"Put him over me and give him the orders. It will amount to the same thing."

Sol thought it over. "All right," he said. "And what must I give *you*?"

"Me?" Sos was taken aback. "I agreed to serve you one year, to earn my name. There is nothing else you need to give me." But he saw Sol's point. If Tyl's loyalty required buttressing, what about his own? Sol was well aware that the training was, in the long run, more important than the discipline of the moment, and he had less hold on Sos than on the others. Theoretically Sos could renounce the name and leave at any time.

"I like your bird," Sol said surprisingly. "Will you give him to me?"

Sos peeked sidewise at the little fellow snoozing on his shoulder. The bird had become so much a part of his life that he hardly thought about the matter any more. "No one owns Stupid. Certainly you have as much claim on him as I do—you were the one who cut down the hawk and saved him. The bird just happened to fix on me, for some reason nobody understands, even though I did nothing for him and tried to shoo him away. I can't give him to you."

"I lost my bracelet in a similar fashion," Sol said, touching his bare wrist.

Sos looked away uncomfortably.

"Yet if I borrowed your bird, and he mated and fathered an egg, I would return that egg to you," Sol murmured.

Sos stomped away, too angry to speak.

No further words passed between them—but the next morning Sol set out again, alone, and Sola stayed at the camp.

Tyl seemed quite satisfied with his promotion. He summoned Sos as soon as the master was out of sight. "I want you to fashion this bunch into the finest fighting force in the area," he said. "Anyone who malingers will answer to me."

Sos nodded and proceeded with his original plan.

First he watched each man practice in the circle, and assessed his style and strengths and weaknesses, making notes on a pad of paper in the script of the ancient texts. Then he ranked the warriors in order, by weapon: first sword, second sword, first staff, and so on. There were twenty swords in the collection; it was the most popular instrument, though the injury and death rate was high. There were sixteen clubs, twelve staffs, ten sticks (he had never discovered why the misnomer 'singlestick' should apply to the pair), five daggers and a solitary star.

The first month consisted entirely of drill within the individual groups, and continual exercise. There was much more of both than the warriors had ever had before, because contestants were readily available and there was no delay or traveling between encounters. Each practiced with his weapon until fatigued, then ran laps around the inner perimeter of the camp and returned for more practice. The best man in each weapon class was appointed leader and told to instruct the others in the fine points of his trade. The original rankings could be altered by challenge from below, so that those whose skill increased could achieve higher standing. There was vigorous competition as they fell into the spirit of it, with spectators from other weapons applauding, jeering and watching to prevent injurious tactics.

The star, in a group of one, practiced with the clubs. The morningstar weapon was an oddity: a short, stout handle with a heavy spiked bail attached by a length of chain. It was a particularly dangerous device; since it lacked control, it was impossible to deliver a gentle blow. The devastating star-ball either struck its target, the points gouging out flesh and bone, or it didn't; it could not be used defensively. The loser of a star vs. star match was often killed or grievously wounded, even in "friendly" matches, and not always by his opponent's strike. Even experienced warriors hesitated to meet an angry starrer in the circle; internecine casualties were too likely.

So it went. The men were hardly aware of general improvement, but Sos saw it and knew that a number of them were turning into very fine artists of battle.

By twos and threes, new men and their families arrived to join the group, sent hither by Sol. They were integrated into the specialty companies and ranked as their skills warranted; the old-timers remarked that the quality of recruits seemed to be descending. By the end of that first month the tribe had swelled to over a hundred fighting men.

At first there were many gawky youngsters, taken only because they were available. Sos had cautioned Sol not to judge by initial skill or appearance. As the training and exercise continued, these youngsters began to fill out and learn the vital nuances of position and pacing, and soon were rising up their respective ladders. Some of the best, Sos suspected, would never have lived long enough to have become really proficient in the normal course; their incorporation into Sol's tribe was their greatest fortune.

Gradually the dissimilar and sometimes surly individuals thrown together by the luck of conquest caught the spirit of the group. A general atmosphere of expectancy developed. It was evident that this was a tribe destined for greater things. Sos picked out the most intelligent men and began instructing them in group tactics: when to fight and when not to fight, and how to come out ahead when the sides seemed even.

"If your group has six good men ranked in order, and you meet a group with six men, each of whom is just a little better than yours, how should you arrange your battle order?" he asked them one day.

"How much better?" Tun wanted to know. He was a clubber, low-ranked because he was too heavy to move quickly.

"Their first man can take your first. Their second can take your second but not your first. Their third can take your third, but not your second or first, and so on down the line."

"I have no one who can beat their first?"

"No one—and he insists on fighting, as do the rest.'"

"But their first will certainly not stand by and let my first overcome a lesser weapon. He will challenge my first, and take him from me. Then their second will do the same to my second . . ."

"Right."

Tun pondered the matter. "The luck of the circle should give me one victory, perhaps two—but I should do best not to meet this tribe."

Tor, the black-bearded sworder, brightened. "I can take five of their men, and lose only my poorest."

"How?" Tun demanded. "Theirs are all better than—"

"I will send my sixth man against their leader, as though he were my best, and keep the rest of my order the same."

"But your first would never agree to fight below your sixth!"

"*My* first will take my orders, even if he thinks they insult him," Tor said. "He will meet their second, and defeat him, and then my second will take their third, and finally my fifth will take their sixth."

"But their first—"

"Will conquer only my sixth—who would have likely lost to any other man. I do not need him."

"And you will have ten men, while he is left with only two," Sos finished. "Yet his team was better than yours, before you fought."

Tun gaped, then laughed, seeing it, for he was not a stupid man. "I will remember that!" he exclaimed. Then he sobered. "Only—what if their best refused to fight any but my best?"

"How is he to know?" Tor demanded.

"How do you know *his* rankings?"

They agreed that the strategy would be effective only with advance scouting, preferably by some experienced but retired warrior. Before long they were all eagerly inventing similar problems and challenging each other for solutions. They fetched dominoes from the game-compartment of the hostel and set them up against each other as tactical situations, the higher values indicating greater proficiency. Tor soon proved to be cleverest at this, and got so that he could parlay almost any random deal into a winning effort. Sos had started this type of competition, but he lost ground to his pupils.

He had shown them how to win with their intelligence when they could not do it by brute force, and he was well satisfied.

The second month, with the physical rankings firmly established, the tribe began inter-weapon competition. The advisors rejoined their own ranks and conspired to overcome all enemies by means of their more subtle skills. Each subgroup now had *esprit de corps* and was eager to demonstrate its superiority over its fellows.

Sos trained men to keep tally: a point for each victory, nothing for each loss. Some laughed to see grown men carrying pencil and pad, emulating scribes among the crazies, and soon the women moved in to take over this task. They prevailed upon Sos to teach them how to write identifications for each group, so that competitive scores could be posted on a public board. Instead he suggested that they learn to make symbols: simplified swords, clubs and other weapons, to be followed by lines slashed in bunches of five for ready comparison. Every day men were to be seen trekking to that board and exclaiming over their victories or bemoaning their losses of rank. As the fives grew too cumbersome with the cumulative totals, the women mastered the more versatile Arabic numerals, and, after them, the men. This was a dividend Sos had not anticipated; the tribe was learning to figure. He walked by one day and spied a little girl adding up her group's daily total on her fingers. Then she took the pencil and posted "56" beside the sword-symbol.

That was when he realized how simple it would be to set up a training course in basic mathematics, and even in full-fledged writing. The nomads were illiterate because they had no reason to read or write. Given that need, the situation

could quickly change. But he was too busy to make anything of it at the time.

The daggers, being the smallest group, were at a disadvantage. Their leader complained to Sos that, even if all five of them won every encounter, they could hardly keep up with the swords, who could lose more than they won and still finish the day with more points. Sos decided that this was a valid objection, so he showed them how to figure on index: the number of points per man. Then he did have to start his class in math, to teach the women how to compute the averages. Sola joined it; she was not the smartest woman available but, since she was alone, she had more time and was able to master the procedures well enough to instruct them. Sos appreciated the help, but her proximity disturbed him. She was too beautiful, and she came too close when he was explaining something.

Strange things happened in the circle. It was discovered that the ranking swords were not necessarily the most effective against the crude clubs, and that those who *could* master clubs might be weak against the staffs. The advisors who first caught on to the need to shift rankings as the type of opposition shifted gained many points for their groups.

Tyl came upon Tor setting out his dominoes in his tent and laughed. Then he saw Tor make notes and call off a marvelously effective battle strategy, and stopped laughing. Tyl, also aloof at first because of the deference he felt due his position, watched the individual progress being made and decided to participate. No one could afford to stand still, and already there were sworders rivaling his prowess. The time even came when he was seen pondering dominoes.

The third month they began doubles drill. Two men had to take the circle against two opponents and defeat them as a team.

"Four men in the circle?" Tyl demanded, shocked. "What charade is this?"

"Ever hear of the tribe of Pit?"

"No."

"A very powerful organization in the far east. They put up their swords by pairs, and their clubs and staffs. They will not enter the circle singly. Do you want them to claim a victory over us by default?"

"No!" And the drill went on.

The daggers and sticks had little trouble, but the staffs could entangle each other and the free-swinging clubs and swords were as likely to injure their partners as their targets. The first day's doubles practice was costly. Again the rankings were shuffled, as the teamed first and second swords found themselves ignominiously defeated by the tenth and fifteenth duo. Why? Because the top-rankers were individualists, while the lower numbers had wisely paired complementary styles: the aggressive but foolhardy offense supported by the staid but certain defense. While the two top sworders lurched against each other and held back strokes because they could not separate friend from foe, the smooth teamwork of the lesser warriors prevailed.

Then inter-group competition again, with reshuffled rankings, and finally mixed doubles: sword paired with club, dagger with staff, until every man could pair with any other weapon against any combination and fight effectively. The scoring had to be revised to match; the women learned fractions and apportioned the sections of the victories where due. Months passed unnoticed as the endless combinations were explored, and an experienced cadre developed to break in the newcomers, naturally bewildered, and show how to improve and ascend the rankings.

The leaves fell, then snow, and the moths and shrews disappeared, though group vigilance and action had long since reduced these menaces to comparative impotence. As a matter of fact, shrew stew had become a staple in the diet, and it was awkward to replace this bountiful source of meat when winter came.

The rings were swept clean each day and the interminable drill went on, in shine or snow. Additional warriors appeared steadily, but still Sol did not return.

8

WITH THE COLD WEATHER, SAV ELECTED TO MOVE INTO THE main tent, which was heated by a perpetual fire. It had been subdivided into numerous smaller compartments, for a certain amount of privacy between families. Increasingly, eligible young women were showing up in search of bracelets. Sav was candid about passing his around.

Sos stayed in the small tent, unwilling to mix freely with those who bore weapons. His impotence in the circle was a matter of increasing distress, though he could not admit it openly. He had not appreciated the extent of his compulsion to assert himself and solve problems by force of arms until denied this privilege.

He had to have a weapon again—but was barred from employing any of the six that the crazies distributed to the cabins. These were mass produced somewhere, standardized and stocked freely in the hostels, and alternates such as the bow and arrows were not useful in the circle.

He had wondered often about this entire state of affairs. Why did the crazies take so much trouble to provide these things, making the nomad existence possible, then affect complete lack of concern for the use men made of them? Sometime he meant to have the answer. Meanwhile he was a member of the battle society, and it was necessary for him to assert himself in its terms.

If he were able.

He stripped his clothing and climbed naked into the warm sleeping bag. This was another item the crazies obligingly stocked in wintertime, and many more than the normal number had been provided at the local cabin, in response to the increased drain on its facilities. They all most certainly knew about this camp, but didn't seem to care. Where the men were, they sent supplies and sought no other controls.

He had a small gas lamp now, which enabled him to read the occasional books the crazies left behind. Even in this regard they were helpful; when he started taking books from the hostel, more appeared, and on the subjects he seemed to favor. He lit the lamp and opened his present volume: a text on farming, pre-Blast style. He tried to read it, but it was complicated and his mind could not concentrate. Type and quantity of fertilizer for specified acreage; crop rotation; pesticide, applications of and cautions concerning . . . such incomprehensible statistifying, when all he wanted to know was how to grow peanuts and carrots. He put the book aside and turned off the light.

It was lonely, now that Sav was gone, and sleep did not come readily. He kept thinking of Sav, passing his bracelet around, embracing yielding and willing flesh, there in the main tent. Sos could have done likewise; there were women who had eyed his own clasp suggestively even though he carried no weapon. He had told himself that his position required that he remain unattached, even for isolated nights. He knew that he deceived himself. Possession of a woman was the other half of manhood, and a warrior could bolster his reputation in that manner as readily as in the circle. The truth was that he refused to take a woman because he was ashamed to do so while weaponless.

Someone was approaching his tent. Possibly Tor, wanting to make a private suggestion. The beard had a good mind and had taken such serious interest in group organization and tactics that he outstripped Sos in this regard. They had become good friends, as far as their special circumstances permitted. Sometimes Sos had eaten with Tor's family, though the contact with plump good-natured Tora and precocious Tori only served to remind him how much he had wanted a family of his own.

Had wanted? It was the other way around. He had never been conscious of the need until recently.

"Sos?"

It was a woman's voice—one he knew too well. "What do you want, Sola?"

Her hooded head showed before the entrance, black against the background snow. "May I come in? It's cold out here."

"It is cold here, too, Sola. Perhaps you should return to your own tent." She, like him, had maintained her own residence, pitched near Tyl's. She had developed an acquaintance with Tyla. She still wore Sol's bracelet, and the men stayed scrupulously clear of her.

"Let me in," she said.

He pulled open the mesh with one bare arm. He had forgotten to let down the solid covering after shutting off the lamp. Sola scrambled in on hands and knees, almost knocking over the lamp, and lay down beside his bag. Sos now dropped the nylon panel, cutting off most of the outside light and, he hoped, heat loss from inside.

"I get so tired, sleeping alone," she said.

"You came here to sleep?"

"Yes."

He had intended the question facetiously and was set back by her answer. A sudden, fierce hope set his pulses thudding, seeming more powerful for its surprise. He had deceived himself doubly: it was neither his position nor his lack of a weapon that inhibited him, but his obsession with one particular woman. This one.

"You want my bracelet?"

"No."

The disappointment was fiercer. "Get out."

"No."

"I will not dishonor another man's bracelet. Or adulterate my own. If you will not leave yourself, I will have you out by force."

"And what if I scream and bring the whole camp running?" Her voice was low.

He remembered encountering a similar situation in his diverse readings, and knew that a man who succumbed to that ploy the first time could never recover his independence of decision. Time would only make it worse. "Scream if you must. You will not stay."

"You would not lay your hands on me," she said smugly, not moving.

He sat up and gripped her furry parka, furious with her and with his guilty longing. The material fell open immediately, wrapped but not fastened. His hand and the filtered light still reflecting in from the snow told him quickly that she wore nothing underneath. No wonder she had been cold!

"It would not look very nice, a naked man struggling in his tent with a naked woman," she said.

"It happens all the time."

"Not when she objects."

"In *my* tent? They would ask why she came naked to it, and did not scream before entering."

"She came dressed, to inquire about a difficult problem. An error in fractions." She fumbled in the pocket and drew out a pad with figures scrawled upon it—he could not see them, but was sure she had done her homework in this respect. Even to the error, one worthy of his attention. "He drew her inside—no, *tricked* her there—then tore off her clothing."

He had fallen rather neatly into her trap after all. She was too well versed. His usefulness to the group would be over, if the alarm were given now. "What do you want?"

"I want to get warm. There is room in your bag for two."

"This will gain you nothing. Are you trying to drive me out?"

"No." She found the zipper and opened the bag, letting the cold air in. In a moment she was lying against him, bare and warm, her parka outside and the zipper refastened.

"Sleep, then." He tried to turn away from her, but the movement only brought them closer together.

She attempted to bring his head over to hers, catching at his hair with one hand, but he was rigid. "Oh, Sos, I did not come to torment you!"

He refused to answer that.

She lay still for a little while, and the burning muliebrity of her laid siege to his resistance. Everything he desired, so close. Available—in the name of dishonor.

Why did she choose this way? She had only to put aside Sol's emblem for a little while. . . .

Another figure detached itself from the shadow of the main tent and trod through the packed snow. Sos could see it, though his eyes were closed, for he recognized the tread. Tor.

"You have your wish. Tor is coming."

Then her bluff stood exposed, for she shrank into the bag and tried to hide. "Send him away!" she whispered.

Sos grabbed the parka and tossed it to the foot of the tent. He drew the lip of the bag over her head, hoping the closure wouldn't suffocate her. He waited.

Tor's feet came up to the tent and stopped. No word was spoken. Then Tor wheeled and departed, evidently deciding that the dark, closed tent meant that his friend was already asleep.

Sola's head emerged when it was safe. "You *do* want me," she said. "You could have embarrassed me. . . ."

"Certainly I want you. Remove his bracelet and take mine, if you want the proof."

"Do you remember when we lay against each other before?" she murmured, this time evading the direct refusal.

"'Greensleeves.'"

"And 'Red River Valley.' And you asked me what I wanted in a man, and I told you leadership."

"You made your choice." He heard the bitterness in his tone.

"But I did not know then what he wanted." She shifted position, placing her free arm under his and around his back and Sos was unable to control the heat of his reaction and knew she knew it.

"You are the leader of this camp," she said. "Everybody knows it, even Tyl. Even Sol. He knew it first of all."

"If you believe that, why do you keep his bracelet?"

"Because I am not a selfish woman!" she flared, amazing him. "He gave me his name when he didn't want to, and I must give him something in return, even if I don't want to. I can't leave him until we are even."

"I don't understand."

It was her turn for bitterness. "You understand!"

"You have a strange system of accounting."

"It is his system, not mine. It doesn't fit into your numbers."

"Why not pick on some other man for your purpose?"

"Because he trusts you—and I love you."

He could offer no rebuttal to that statement. Sol had made the original offer, not her.

"I will leave now, if you ask me," she whispered. "No screaming, no trouble, and I will not come again."

She could not afford the gesture. She had already won. Wordlessly he clasped her and sought her lips and body.

And now she held back. "You know the price?"

"I know the price."

Then she was as eager as he.

9

IN THE SPRING SOL REAPPEARED, LEAN AND SCARRED AND SOLEMN, toting his barrow. More than two hundred men were there to greet him, tough and eager to the last. They knew his return meant action for them all.

He listened to Tyl's report and nodded matter-of-factly. "We march tomorrow," he said.

That night Sav came to share his tent again. It occurred to Sos that the staffer's departure and return had been remarkably convenient, but he did not comment directly. "Your bracelet got tired?"

"I like to keep moving. 'Bout run out of ground."

"Can't raise much of a family that way."

"Sure can't!" Sav agreed. "Anyway, I need my strength. I'm second staff now."

Yes, he thought forlornly. The first had become second, and there was nothing to do but abide by it. The winter had been warmer than the spring.

The tribe marched. The swords, fifty strong, moved out first, claiming their privilege as eventual winners of the point-score tournament. The daggers followed, winners on index, and then the sticks, staffs and clubs. The lone morningstar brought up the rear, low scorer but not put out. "My weapon is not for games," he said, with some justice.

Sol no longer fought. He stayed with Sola, showing unusual concern for her welfare, and let the fine military machine Sos had fashioned operate with little overt direction. Did he know what his wife had been doing all winter? He had to, for Sola was pregnant.

Tyl ran the tribe. When they encountered a single man who was willing to come to terms, Tyl gave the assignment to the group corresponding to the man's weapon and let the leader of that group select a representative to enter the circle. The advantage of the extended training quickly showed: the appointed warriors were generally in better physical shape than their opponents and superior strategists, and almost always won. When they lost, more often than not the victor, perceiving the size and power of the tribe, challenged the group leader in order to be incorporated into it. Tyl allowed no one to travel with the tribe who was not bound to it.

Only Sos was independent—and he wished he were not.

A week out they caught up to another tribe. It contained about forty men, and its leader was typical of the crafty oldsters Sos had anticipated. The man met Tyl and surveyed the situation—and agreed to put up just four warriors for the circle: sword, staff, sticks and club. He refused to risk more.

Disgruntled, Tyl retired for a conference with Sos. "It's a small tribe, but he has many good men. I can tell they are experienced and capable by the way they move and the nature of their scars."

"And perhaps also by the report of our advance scouts," Sos murmured.

"He won't even send his best against us!" Tyl said indignantly.

"Put up fifty men and challenge him yourself for his entire group. Let him inspect the men and satisfy himself that they are worth his trouble."

Tyl smiled and went to obtain Sol's official approval, a formality only. In due course he had forty-five assorted warriors assembled.

"Won't work." Tor muttered.

The wily tribemaster looked over the offerings, grunting with approval. "Good men," he agreed. Then he contemplated Tyl. "Aren't you the man of two weapons?"

"Sword and stick."

"You used to travel alone—and now you are second in command to a tribe of two hundred."

"That's right."

"I will not fight you."

"You insist upon meeting our master Sol?"

"Certainly not!"

Tyl controlled his temper with obvious difficulty and turned to Sos. "What now, advisor?" he demanded with irony.

"Now you take Tor's advice." Sos didn't know what the beard had in mind, but suspected it would work.

"I think his weak spot is his pride," Tor said conspiratorially. "He won't fight if he thinks he might lose, and he won't put up more than a few men at a time, so he can quit as soon as the wind blows against him. No profit for us there. But if we can make him look ridiculous—"

"Marvelous!" Sos exclaimed, catching on. "We'll pick up four jokers and shame him into a serious entry!"

"And we'll assign a core of chucklers. The loudest mouths we have."

"And we have plenty," Sos agreed, remembering the quality of heckling that had developed during the intense inter-group competition.

Tyl shrugged dubiously. "You handle it. I want no part of this." He went to his tent.

"He really wanted to fight himself," Tor remarked. "But he's out. He never laughs."

They compared notes and decided upon a suitable quartet for the circle. After that they rounded up an even more special group of front-row spectators.

The first match began at noon. The opposing sworder strode up to the circle, a tall, serious man somewhat beyond the first flush of youth. From Sol's ranks came Dal, the second dagger: a round-faced, short-bodied man whose frequent laugh sounded more like a giggle. He was not a very good fighter overall, but the intense practice had shown up his good point: he had never been defeated by the sword. No one quite fathomed this odd-ity, since a stout man was generally most vulnerable to sharp instruments, but it had been verified many times over.

The sworder stared dourly at his opponent, then stepped into the circle and stood on-guard. Dal drew one of his knives and faced him—precociously imitating with the eight-inch blade the formal stance of the other. The picked watchers laughed.

More perplexed than angry, the sworder feinted experimentally. Dal countered with the diminutive knife as

though it were a full-sized sword. Again the audience laughed, more boisterously than strictly necessary.

Sos aimed a surreptitious glance at the other tribe's master. The man was not at all amused.

Now the sworder attacked in earnest, and Dal was obliged to draw his sec-ond dagger—daintily—and hold off the heavier weapon with quick feints and maneuvers. A pair of daggers were gen-erally considered to be no match for a sword unless the wielder were extremely agile. Dal looked quite *un*agile—but his round body always happened to be just a hair out of the sword's path, and he was quick to take advantage of the openings created by the sword's inertia. No one who faced the twin blades in the circle could afford to forget that there were two, and that the bearer had to be held at a safe distance at all times. It was use-less to block a single knife if the second were on its way to a vulnerable target.

Had the sworder been a better man, the tactics would have been foolhardy; but again and again Dal was able to send his opponent lumbering awkwardly past, wide open for a crippling stab. Dal didn't stab. Instead he flicked off a lock of the sworder's hair and waved it about like a tassel while the picked audience roared. He slit the back of the sworder's panta-loons, forcing him to grab them hastily, while Sol's men rolled on the ground, yanked up their own trunks and slapped each other on shoulders and backs.

Finally the man tripped over Dal's art-ful foot and fell out of the circle, igno-miniously defeated. But Dal didn't leave the circle. He kept on feinting and flip-ping his knives as though unaware that his opponent was gone.

The opposite master watched with frozen face.

Their next was the staffer. Against him Tor had sent the sticks, and the performance was a virtual duplicate of the first. Kin the Sticker fenced ludicrously with one hand while carrying the alternate singlestick under his arm, in his teeth or between his legs, to the lewd glee of the scoffers. He managed to make the staffer look inept and untrained, though the man was neither. Kin beat a tattoo against the staff, as though playing music, and bent down to pepper the man's feet painfully. By this time even some of the warriors of the other tribe were chuckling . . . but not their chief.

The third match was the reverse: Sav met the sticks. He hummed a merry folksong as he poked the slightly bulky belly of his opposite with the end of his staff, preventing him from getting close. "Swing low, sweet chariot!" he sang as he jabbed. The man had to take both sticks in one hand in order to make a grab for the staff with the other. "Oh, no John, no John, no John, no!" Sav caroled as he wrapped that double hand and sent both sticks flying.

It was not his name, but that man was ever after to be known in the tribe as Jon.

Against their club went Mok the Morningstar. He charged into the circle whirling the terrible spiked ball over his head so that the wind sang through the spikes, and when the club blocked it the chain wrapped around the hand until the orbiting ball came up tight against the clubber's hand and crushed it painfully. Mok yanked, and the club came away, while the man looked at his bleeding fingers. As the star had claimed: his was not a weapon for games.

Mok caught the club, reversed it, and offered the handle to his opponent with a bow. "You have another hand," he said courteously. "Why waste it while good bones remain?" The man stared at him and backed out of the circle, utterly humbled. The last fight was over.

The other master was almost incoherent. "Never have I seen such—such—"

"What did you expect from the buffoons you sent against us?" a slim, baby-faced youngster replied, leaning against his sword. He had been foremost among the scoffers though he hardly looked big enough to heft his weapon. "*We* came to fight, but your cavorting clowns—"

"You!" the master cried out furiously. "You meet my first sword, then!"

The boy looked frightened. "But you said only four—"

"No! All my men will fight. But first I want you—and that foul beard next to you. And those two loudmouthed clubbers!"

"Done!" the boy cried, standing up and running to the circle. It was Neq, despite his youth and diminutive stature the fourth sword of fifty.

The beard, of course, was clever Tor himself, now third sword. The two clubbers were first and second in their group of thirty-seven.

At the end of the day Sol's tribe was richer by some thirty men.

Sol pondered the matter for a day. He talked with Tyl and thought some more. Finally he summoned Sos and Tor: "This dishonors the circle," he said. "We fight to win or lose, not to laugh."

Then he sent Sos after the other master to apologize and offer a serious return match, but the man had had enough. "Were you not weaponless, I would split your head in the circle!" he said.

So it went. The group's months in the badlands camp had honed it to a superb fighting force, and the precise multi-weapon ranking system placed the warriors exactly where they could win. There were some losses—but these were overwhelmingly compensated by the gains. Upon occasion Tyl had the opportunity to take the circle against a master, matching a selected subtribe equivalent to the other tribe, as he had wanted to do the first time. Twice he won, bringing a total of seventy warriors into Sol's group, much to his pride . . . and once he lost.

That was when Sol came out of his apparent retirement to place his entire tribe of over three hundred men against the fifty—now one hundred—belonging to the victor and challenged for it all. He took the sword and killed the other master in as ruthless and businesslike an attack as Sos had ever seen. Tor made notes on the technique, so as to call them out as pointers for the sword group. Tyl kept his ranking—and if he had ever dreamed of replacing Sol, it was certain that the vision perished utterly that day.

Only once was the tribe seriously balked, and not by another tribe. One day an enormous, spectacularly muscled man came ambling down the trail swinging his club as though it were a single-stick. Sos was actually one of the largest men in the group, but the stranger was substantially taller and broader through the shoulders than he. This was Bog, whose disposition was pleasant, whose intellect was scant, and whose chiefest joy was pulverizing men in the circle.

Fight? "Good, good!" he exclaimed, smiling broadly. "One, two, three a'time! Okay!" And he bounded into the circle and awaited all comers. Sos had the impression that the main reason the man had failed to specify more at a time was that he could count no higher.

Tyl, his curiosity provoked, sent in the first club to meet him. Bog launched into battle with no apparent science. He simply swept the club back and forth with such ferocity that his opponent was helpless against it. Hit or miss, Bog continued unabated, fairly bashing the other out of the circle before the man could catch his footing.

Victorious, Bog grinned. "More!" he cried.

Tyl looked at the tribe's erstwhile first clubber, a man who had won several times in the circle. He frowned, not quite believing it. He sent in the second club.

The same thing happened. Two men lay stunned on the ground, thoroughly beaten.

Likewise the two ranking swords and a staff, in quick order. "More!" Bog exclaimed happily, but Tyl had had enough. Five top men were shaken and lost, in the course of only ten minutes, and the victor hardly seemed to be tired.

"Tomorrow," he said to the big clubber.

"Okay!" Bog agreed, disappointed, and accepted the hospitality of the tribe for the evening. He polished off two full-sized meals and three willing women before he retired for the night. Male and female alike gaped at his respective appetites, hardly able to credit either department, but these were not subject to refutation. Bog conquered everything—one, two or three at a time.

Next day he was as good as ever. Sol was on hand this time to watch while Bog bashed club, sticks and daggers with equal facility, and even flattened the terrible star. When struck, he paid no attention, though some blows were cruel; when cut, he licked the blood like a tiger and laughed. Blocking him was no good; he had such power that no really effective inhibition was practical. "More!" he cried after each debacle, and he never tired.

"We must have that man," Sol said.

"We have no one to take him," Tyl objected. "He has already wiped out nine of our best, and hasn't even felt the competition. I might kill him with the sword—but I couldn't defeat him bloodlessly. We'd have no use for him dead."

"He must be met with the club," Sos said. "That's the only thing with the mass to slow him. A powerful, agile, durable club."

Tyl stared meaningfully at the three excellent clubbers seated by Bog's side of the circle. All wore large bandages where flesh and bone had succumbed to the giant's attack. "If those were our ranked instruments, we need an unranked warrior," he observed.

"Yes," Sol said. He stood up.

"Wait a minute!" both men cried. "Don't chance it yourself," Sos added. "You have too much to risk."

"The day any man conquers me with any weapon," Sol said seriously, "is the day I go to the mountain." He took up his club and walked to the circle.

"The master!" Bog cried, recognizing him. "Good fight?"

"He didn't even settle terms," Tyl groaned. "This is nothing more than man-to-man."

"Good fight," Sol agreed, and stepped inside.

Sos concurred. In the headlong drive for empire, it seemed a culpable waste to chance Sol in the circle for anything less than a full tribe. Accidents were always possible. But they had already learned that their leader had other things on his mind these days than his empire. Sol proved his manhood by his battle prowess, and he could allow no slightest question there, even in his own mind. He had continued his exercises regularly, keeping his body toned.

Perhaps it took a man without a weapon to appreciate just how deeply the scars of the other kind of deprivation went.

Bog launched into his typical windmill attack, and Sol parried and ducked expertly. Bog was far larger, but Sol was faster and cut off the ferocious arcs before they gained full momentum. He ducked under one swing and caught Bog on the side of the head with the short, precise flick Sos had seen him demonstrate before. The club was not clumsy or slow in Sol's hand.

The giant absorbed the blow and didn't seem to notice. He bashed away without hesitation, smiling. Sol had to back away and dodge cleverly to avoid being driven out of the circle, but Bog followed him without letup.

Sol's strategy was plain. He was conserving his strength, letting the other expend his energies uselessly. Whenever there was an opening, he sneaked his own club in to bruise head, shoulder or stomach, weakening the man further. It was a good policy—except that Bog refused to be weakened. "Good!" he grunted when Sol scored—and swung again.

Half an hour passed while the entire tribe massed around the arena, amazed. They all knew Sol's competence; what they couldn't understand was Bog's indefatigable power. The club was a solid weapon, heavier with every swing, and prolonged exercise with it inevitably deadened the arm, yet Bog never slowed or showed strain. Where did he get such stamina?

Sol had had enough of the waiting artifice. He took the offense. Now he laid about him with swings like Bog's, actually forcing the bigger man to take defensive measures. It was the first time they had seen it; for all they had known until that point, Bog *had* no defense, since he had never needed it. As it was, he was not good at it, and soon got smashed full force across the side of the neck.

Sos rubbed his own neck with sympathetic pain, seeing the man's hair flop out and spittle fly from his open mouth. The blow should have laid him out for the rest of the day. It didn't. Bog hesitated momentarily, shook his head, then grinned. "Good!" he said—and smote mightily with his own weapon.

Sol was sweating profusely, and now took the defensive stance from necessity. Again he fended Bog off with astute maneuvers, while the giant pressed the attack as vigorously as before. Sol had not yet been whacked upon head or torso; his defense was too skilled for the other to penetrate. But neither could he shake his opponent or wear him down.

After another half hour he tried again, with no better effect. Bog seemed to be impervious to physical damage. After that Sol was satisfied to wait.

"What's the record for club-club?" someone asked.

"Thirty-four minutes," another replied.

The timer Tor had borrowed from the hostel indicated a hundred and four minutes. "It isn't possible to keep that pace indefinitely," he said.

The shadows lengthened. The contest continued.

Sos, Tyl and Tor huddled with the other advisors. "They're going on until dark!" Tor exclaimed incredulously. "Sol won't quit, and Bog doesn't know how."

"We have to break this up before they *both* drop dead," Sos said.

"How?"

That was the crux. They were sure neither participant would quit voluntarily, and the end was not in view. Bog's strength seemed boundless, and Sol's determination and skill matched it. Yet the onset of night would multiply the chances for a fatal culmination, that nobody wanted. The battle would have to be stopped.

It was a situation no one had imagined, and they could think of no ethical way to handle it. In the end, they decided to stretch the circle code a bit.

The staff squad took the job. A phalanx of them charged into the circle, walling off the combatants and carrying them away. "Draw!" Sav yelled. "Tie! Impasse! Even! No decision!"

Bog picked himself up, confused.

"Supper!" Sos yelled at him. "Sleep! Women!"

That did it. "Okay!" the monster clubber agreed.

Sol thought about it, contemplating the extended shadows. "All right," he said at last.

Bog went over to shake hands. "You pretty good, for little guy," he said graciously. "Next time we start in morning, okay? More day."

"Okay!" Sol agreed, and everyone laughed.

That night Sola rubbed liniment into Sol's arms and legs and back and put him away for a good twelve hours' exhaustion. Bog was satisfied with one oversized meal and one sturdy well-upholstered lass. He disdained medication for his purpling bruises. "Good fight!" he said, contented.

The following day he went his way, leaving behind the warriors he had conquered. "Only for fun!" he explained. "Good, good."

They watched him disappear down the trail, singing tunelessly and flipping his club end-over-end in the air.

10

"MY YEAR IS UP," SOS SAID. "I would have you stay," Sol replied slowly. "You have given good service."

"You have five hundred men and an elite corps of advisors. You don't need me."

Sol looked up and Sos was shocked to see tears in his eyes. "I do need you," he said. "I have no other friend."

Sos did not know what to say.

Sola joined them, hugely pregnant. Soon she would travel to a crazy hospital for delivery. "Perhaps you have a son," Sos said.

"When you find what you need, come back," Sol told him, accepting the inevitable.

"I will." That was all they could say to each other.

He left the camp that afternoon, traveling east. Day by day the landscape became more familiar as he approached the region of his childhood. He skirted the marked badlands near the coast, wondering what mighty cities had stood where the silent death radiated now, and whether there would ever be such massive assemblages of people again. The books claimed that nothing green had grown in the centers of these encampments, that concrete and asphalt covered the ground between buildings and made the landscape as flat as the surface of a lake, that machines like those the crazies used today had been everywhere, doing everything. Yet all had vanished in the Blast. Why? There were many unanswered questions.

A month of hiking brought him to the school he had attended before beginning his travels as a warrior. Only a year and a half had elapsed, but already it had become an entirely different facet of his existence, one now unfamiliar to him and strange to see again. Still, he knew his way around.

He entered the arched front doorway and walked down the familiar, foreign hall to the door at the end marked "Principal." A girl he did not remember sat at the desk. He decided she was a recent graduate, pretty, but very young. "I'd like to see Mr. Jones," he said, pronouncing the obscure name carefully.

"And who is calling?" She stared at Stupid, perched as ever upon his shoulder.

"Sos," he said, then realized that the name would mean nothing here. "A former student. He knows me."

She spoke softly into an intercom and listened for the reply. "Doctor Jones will see you now," she said, and smiled at him as though he were not a ragged-bearded, dirt-encrusted pagan with a mottled bird on his shoulder.

He returned the gesture, appreciating her attention though he knew it was professional, and went on through the inner door.

The principal rose immediately and came around the desk to greet him. "Yes of course I remember you! Class of '107, and you stayed to practice with the—the sword, wasn't it? What do you call yourself now?"

"Sos." He knew Jones knew it already, and was simply offering him the chance to explain the change. He didn't take it immediately, and the principal, experienced in such matters, came to his rescue again.

"Sos. Beautiful thing, that three-letter convention. Wish I knew how it originated. Well, sit down, Sos, and tell me everything. Where did you acquire your pet? That's a genuine mock-sparrow, if I haven't lost my eye for badlands fauna." A very gentle fatherly inflection came into his voice. "You have been poking into dangerous regions, warrior. Are you back to stay?"

"I don't know. I don't think so. I—I don't know where my loyalties lie, now." How rapidly he resumed the mood of adolescence, in this man's presence.

"Can't make up your mind whether you're sane or crazy, eh?" Jones said, and laughed in his harmless way. "I know it's a hard decision. Sometimes I still wish I could chuck it all and take up one of those glamorous weapons and—you didn't kill anybody, I hope?"

"No. Not directly, anyway," he said, thinking of the recalcitrant dagger Nar and Tyl's execution of him. "I only fought a few times, and always for little things. The last time was for my name."

"Ah, I see. No more than that?"

"And perhaps for a woman, too."

"Yes. Life isn't always so simple in the simple world, is it? If you care to amplify—"

Sos recounted the entire experience he had had, the emotional barriers overcome at last, while Jones listened sympathetically. "I see," the principal said at the end. "You do have a problem." He cogitated for a moment—"thought" seemed too simple a word to apply to him—then touched the intercom. "Miss Smith, will you check the file on one 'Sol,' please? S-O-L. Probably last year, no, two years ago, west coast. Thank you."

"Did he go to school?" Sos had never thought of this.

"Not here, certainly. But we have other training schools, and he sounds as though he's had instruction. Miss Smith will check it out with the computer. There just might be something on the name."

They waited for several minutes, Sos increasingly uncomfortable as he reminded himself that he should have cleaned up before coming here. The crazies had something of a fetish about dirt: they never went long without removing it. Perhaps it was because they tended to stay within their buildings and machines, where aromas could concentrate.

"The girl," he said, filling time, "Miss Smith—is she a student?"

Jones smiled tolerantly. "No longer. I believe she is actually a year older than you are. We can't be certain because she was picked up running wild near one of the radioactive areas a number of years ago and we never did manage to trace her parentage. She was trained at another unit, but you can be sure there was a change in her, er, etiquette. Underneath, I daresay, there is nomad yet, but she's quite competent."

It was hard to imagine that such a polished product was forest-born, even though he had been through it himself. "Do you really get all your people from—"

"From the real world? Very nearly, Sos. I was a sword-bearer myself, thirty years ago."

"A sworder? You?"

"I'll assume that your astonishment is complimentary. Yes, I fought in the circle. You see—"

"I have it, Dr. Jones," the intercom said. "S.O.L. Would you like me to read it off?"

"Please."

"Sol—adopted code name for mutilated foundling, testes transplant, insulin therapy, comprehensive manual training, discharged from San Francisco orphanage B107. Do you want the details on that, Dr. Jones?"

"No thanks. That will do nicely, Miss Smith." He returned to Sos. "That may not be entirely clear to you. It seems your friend was an orphan. There was some trouble, I remember, about fifteen years ago on the west coast and, well, we had to pick up the pieces. Families wiped out, children tortured—this type of thing will happen occasionally when you're dealing with primitives. Your Sol was castrated at the age of five and left to bleed to death . . . well, he was one of the ones we happened to catch in time. A transplant operation took care of the testosterone, and insulin shock therapy helped eradicate the traumatic memories, but, well, there's only so much we can do. Evidently he wasn't suited to intellectual stimulation, as you were, so he received manual instead. From what you told me, it was exceptionally effective. He seems to have adjusted well."

"Yes." Sos was beginning to understand things about Sol that had baffled him before. Orphaned at a vulnerable age by tribal savagery, he would naturally strive to protect himself most efficiently and to abolish all men and all tribes that might pose a personal threat. Raised in an orphanage he would seek friendship—and not know how to recognize it or what to do with it. And he would want a family his own, that he would protect fanatically. How much more precious a child—to the man who could never father one!

Couple this background with a physical dexterity and endurance amounting to genius, and there was—Sol.

"Why do you do all this?" Sos asked. "I mean, building hostels and stocking them, training children, marking off the badlands, projecting television programs. You get no thanks for it. You know what they call you."

"Those who desire nonproductive danger and glory are welcome to it," Jones said. "Some of us prefer to live safer, more useful lives. It's all a matter of temperament, and that can change with age."

"But you could have it all for yourselves! If—if you did not feed and clothe the warriors, they would perish."

"That's good enough reason to continue service, then, don't you think?"

Sos shook his head. "You aren't answering my question."

"I can't answer it. In time you will answer it for yourself. Then perhaps you will join us. Meanwhile, we're always ready to help in whatever capacity we are able."

"How can you help a man who wants a weapon when he has sworn to carry none, and who loves a woman who is pledged to another man?"

Jones smiled again. "Forgive me, Sos, if these problems appear transitory to me. If you look at it objectively, I think you'll see that there *are* alternatives."

"Other women, you mean? I know that 'Miss' you put on your receptionist's name means she is looking for a husband, but I just don't find it in me to be reasonable in quite that way. I was willing to give any girl a fair trial by the bracelet, just as I gave any man fair battle in that circle, but somehow all my preferences have been shaped to Sola's image. And she loves me, too."

"That seems to be the way love is," Jones agreed regretfully. "But if I understand the situation correctly, she will go with you, after her commitment to Sol is finished. I would call this a rather mature outlook on her part."

"She *won't* just 'go' with me! She wants a name with prestige, and I don't even carry a weapon."

"Yet she recognized your true importance in the tribe. Are you sure it isn't your own desire, more than hers? To win a battle reputation, that is?"

"I'm not sure at all," Sos admitted. His position, once stated openly, sounded much less reasonable than before.

"So it all comes down to the weapon. But you did not swear to quit *all* weapons—only the six standard ones."

"Same thing, isn't it?"

"By no means. There have been hundreds of weapons in the course of Earth's history. We standardized on six for convenience, but we can also provide prototype nonstandard items, and if any ever became popular we could negotiate for mass production. For example, you employed the straight sword with basket hilt, patterned after medieval models, though of superior grade, of course. But there is also the scimitar—the curved blade—and the rapier, for fencing. The rapier doesn't look as impressive as the broadsword, but it is probably a more deadly weapon in confined quarters, such as your battle circle. We could—"

"I gave up the sword in all its forms. I don't care to temporize or quibble about definitions."

"I suspected you would feel that way. So you rule out any variation of blade, club or stick?"

"Yes."

"And we rule out pistols, blowguns and boomerangs—anything that acts at a distance or employs a motive power other than the arm of the wielder. We allow the bow and arrow for hunting—but that wouldn't be much good in the circle anyway."

"Which pretty well covers the field."

"Oh, no, Sos. Man is more inventive than that, particularly when it comes to modes of destruction. Take the whip, for example—usually thought of as a punitive instrument, but potent as a weapon too. That's a long fine thong attached to a short handle. It is possible to stand back and slash the shirt off a man's back with mere flicks of the wrist, or to pinion his arm and jerk him off balance, or snap out an eye. Very nasty item, in the experienced hand."

"How does it defend against the smash of the club?"

"Much as the daggers do, I'm afraid. The whipper just has to stay out of the club's way."

"I would like to defend myself as well as to attack." But Sos was gaining confidence that some suitable weapon for him did exist. He had not realized that Jones knew so much about the practical side of life. Wasn't it really for some such miracle he had found his way here?

"Perhaps we shall have to improvise." Jones tugged a piece of string between his fingers. "A net would be fine defensively, but—" His eyes continued to focus on the string as his expression became intent. "That may well be it!"

"String?"

"The garrote. A length of cord used to strangle a man. Quite effective, I assure you."

"But how would I get close enough to a dagger to strangle him, without getting disemboweled? And it still wouldn't stop a sword or club."

"A long enough length of it would. Actually, I am visualizing something more like a chain—flexible, but hard enough to foil a blade and heavy enough to entangle a club. A—a metal rope, perhaps. Good either offensively or defensively, I'm sure."

"A rope." Sos tried to imagine it as a weapon, but failed.

"Or a bolas," Jones said, carried away by his line of thought. "Except that you would not be allowed to throw the entire thing, of course. Still, weighted ends—come down to the shop and we'll see what we can work up."

Miss Smith smiled at him again as they passed her, but Sos pretended not to notice. She had a very nice smile, and her hair was set in smooth light waves, but she was nothing like Sola.

That day Sos gained a weapon—but it was five months before he felt proficient enough with it to undertake the trail again.

Miss Smith did not speak to him at the termination, but Jones bid him farewell sadly. "It was good to have you back with us if only for these few months, Sos. If things don't work out—"

"I don't know," Sos said, still unable to give him a commitment. Stupid chirped.

11

AS HE HAD BEGUN TWO YEARS BEFORE, SOS SET OUT TO FIND his fortune. Then he had become Sol the Sword, not suspecting what his alliteratively chosen name would bring him to; now he was Sos the Rope. Then he had fought in the circle for pleasure and reputation and minor differences; now he fought to perfect his technique. Then he had taken his women as they came; now he dreamed of only one.

Yet there were things about the blonde Miss Smith that could have intrigued him, in other circumstances. She was literate, for one thing, and that was something he seldom encountered in the nomad world. True, she was of the crazies' establishment—but she would have left it, had he asked her to; that much had become apparent. He had not asked . . . and now, briefly, he wondered whether he had made a mistake.

He thought of Sola and that wiped out all other fancies.

Where was Sol's tribe now? He had no idea. He could only wander until he got word of it, then follow until he caught up, sharpening his skill in that period. He had a weapon now, and with it he meant to win his bride.

The season was early spring, and the leaf-buds were just beginning to form. As always at this time of year, the men brought their families to the cabins, not anxious to pitch small tents against the highly variable nights. The young single girls came, too, seeking their special conquests. Sos merged with these groups in crowded camaraderie, sleeping on the floor when necessary, declining to share a bunk if it meant parting with his bracelet, and conversing with others on sundry subjects. Sol's tribe? No—no one knew its present whereabouts, though some had heard of it. Big tribe—a thousand warriors, wasn't it? Maybe he should ask one of the masters; they generally kept track of such things.

The second day out Sos engaged in a status match with a sticker. The man had questioned whether a simple length of rope could be seriously considered a weapon, and Sos had offered to demonstrate, in friendly fashion. Curious bystanders gathered around as the two men entered the circle

Sos's intensive practice had left his body in better condition than ever before. He had thought he had attained his full growth two years ago, but the organs and flesh of his body had continued to change, slowly. Indeed, he seemed to be running more and more to muscle, and today was a flat solid

man of considerable power. He wondered sometimes whether he *had* been touched by radiation, and whether it could act in this fashion.

He was ready, physically—but it had been a long time since he took the circle with a weapon. His hands became sweaty, and he suddenly felt unsure of himself, a stranger in this ring of physical decision. Could he still fight? He had to; all his hopes depended upon this.

His rope was a slender metallic cord twenty-five feet long, capped and weighted at either end. He wore it coiled about his shoulders when traveling, and it weighed several pounds.

Stupid had learned to watch the rope. Sos loosened several feet of it and held a slack loop in one hand as he faced the other man, and Stupid quickly made for a nearby tree. The two sticks glinted as the other attacked, the right beating at his head while the left maintained a defensive guard. Sos jumped clear, bounding to the far side of the circle. His nervousness vanished as the action began, and he knew he was all right. His rope shot out as the man advanced again, entangling the offensive wrist. A yank, and the sticker was pulled forward, stumbling.

Sos jerked expertly and the cord fell free, just as he had practiced it, and snapped back to his waiting hand. The man was on him again, directing quick blows with both sticks so that a single throw could not interfere with the pair. Sos flipped a central loop over the sticker's neck, ducked under his arm and leaped for the far side of the ring again. The loop tightened, choking the man and pulling him helplessly backward.

Another jerk and the rope fell free again. Sos could have kept it taut and finished the fight immediately, but he preferred to make a point. He wanted to prove, to others and to himself, that the rope could win in a number of guises—and to discover any weaknesses in it before he had a serious encounter.

The sticker approached more cautiously the third time, keeping one arm high to ward off the snaking rope. The man knew now that the coil was an oddity but no toy; a weapon to be wary of. He jumped in suddenly, thinking to score a blow by surprise—and Sos smacked him blindingly across the forehead with the end.

The man reeled back, grasping the fact of defeat. A red welt appeared just above his eyes, and it was obvious that the rope could have struck an inch lower and done terrible damage, had Sos chosen so. As it was, his eyes watered profusely, and the sticker had to strike out almost randomly.

Sos let down his guard, looking for a kind way to finish the encounter—and the man happened to connect with hard rap to the side of his head. The single-stick was no club, but still could easily knock out a man, and Sos was momentarily shaken. His opponent followed up with the other stick immediately, raining blows upon head and shoulders before Sos could plunge away.

He *had* been away from the circle too long! He should never have eased his own attack. He was fortunate that the other was operating on reflex rather than calculated skill and had struck without proper aim. He had his lesson, and he would not forget it.

Sos stayed away until his head was clear, then set about finishing it. He wrapped the rope about the man's legs,

lassoing them, and yanked the feet from under. He bent over the sticker, this time bunching his shoulders to absorb the ineffective blows, and pinioned both arms with a second loop. He gripped the coils with both hands strategically placed, lifted, and heaved.

The man came up, hogtied and helpless. Sos whirled him around in a complete arc and let go. The body flew out of the ring and landed on the lawn beyond the gravel. He had not been seriously hurt, but was completely humiliated.

The rope had proven itself in combat.

The following weeks established Sos as a reputable fighter against other weapons as well. His educated rope quickly snared the hand that wielded sword or club, defending by incapacitating the offense, and the throttle-coil kept the flashing hands of the dagger away. Only against the staff did he have serious trouble. The long pole effectively prevented him from looping the hands, since it extended the necessary range for a lasso enormously and tended to tangle his rope and slow alternate attacks. Wherever he flung, there was the length of rigid metal, blocking him. But the staff was mainly a defensive weapon, which gave him time to search out an opening and prevail. He made a mental note, however: never tackle the quarterstaff when in a hurry.

Still there was no positive word on Sol's tribe. It was as though it had disappeared, though he was certain this was not the case. Finally he took the advice offered the first night and sought the nearest major tribe.

This happened to be the Pit doubles. He was not at all sure that their leader would give information to an isolated warrior merely because he asked for it. The Pit master had a reputation for being surly and secretive. But Sos had no partner to make a doubles challenge for information, and none of the men he had met were ones he cared to trust his life to in the circle.

He gave a mental shrug and set course for the Pit encampment. He would dodge that obstacle when he came to it.

Three days later he met a huge clubber ambling in the opposite direction, tossing his weapon into the air and humming tunelessly. Sos stopped, surprised, but there was no doubt.

It was Bog, the indefatigable swinger who had battered Sol for half a day, for the sheer joy of fighting.

"Bog!" he cried.

The giant stopped, not recognizing him. "Who you?" he demanded, pointing the club.

Sos explained where they had met. "Good fight!" Bog exclaimed, remembering Sol. But he did not know or care where Sol's tribe had gone.

"Why not travel with me?" Sos asked him, thinking of the Pit doubles. To team with such a man—! "I'm looking for Sol. Maybe we can find him together. Maybe another good fight."

"Okay!" Bog agreed heartily. "You come with me."

"But I want to inquire at the Pit's. You're going the wrong way."

Bog did not follow the reasoning. "My way," he said firmly, hefting the club.

Sos could think of only one way to budge him—a dangerous way. "I'll fight you for it. I win, we go my way. Okay?"

"Okay!" he agreed with frightening enthusiasm. The prospect of a fight always swayed Bog.

Sos had to backtrack two hours' journey to reach the nearest circle, and by that time it was late afternoon. The giant was eager to do battle, however.

"All right—but we quit at dusk."

"Okay!" And they entered the circle as people rushed up to witness the entertainment. Some had seen Bog fight before, or heard of him, and others had encountered Sos. There was considerable speculation about the outcome of this unusual match. Most of it consisted of estimates of the number of minutes or seconds it would require for Bog to take the victory.

It was fully as bad as he had feared. Bog blasted away with his club, heedless of obstructions. Sos ducked and weaved and backpedaled, feeling naked without a solid weapon, knowing that sooner or later the ferocious club would catch up to him. Bog didn't seem to realize that his blows hurt his opponents; to him, it was all sport.

Sos looped the arm with a quick throw—and Bog swung without change of pace, yanking the rope and Sos after him. The man had incredible power! Sos dropped the garrote over his head and tightened it behind the tremendous neck—and Bog kept swinging, unheeding, the muscles lining that column so powerful that he could not be choked.

The spectators gaped, but Bog was not even aware of them. Sos saw a couple of them touch their necks and knew they were marveling at Bog's invulnerability. Sos gave up the choke and concentrated on Bog's feet, looping them together when he had the chance and yanking. The big man simply stood there, legs spread, balanced by the backlash of his own swings, and caught the taut rope with a mash that ripped the other end from Sos's hands painfully.

By the time he recovered it, Bog was free, still swinging gleefully. Sos had managed to avoid anything more serious than grazing blows—but these were savage enough. It was only a matter of time, unless he retreated from the circle before getting tagged.

He could not give up! He needed this man's assistance, and he had to ascertain that his weapon was effective against a top warrior as well as the mediocre ones. He decided upon one desperate stratagem.

Sos looped, not Bog's arm, but the club itself, catching it just above the handle. Instead of tightening the coil, however, he let it ride, keeping the rope slack as he ducked under the motion. As he did so, he dropped the rest of the rope to the ground, placed both feet upon it, and shifted his full weight to rest there.

As the club completed its journey the rope snapped taut. Sos was jerked off his feet by the yank—but the club received an equal shock, right at the moment least expected by the wielder. It twisted in Bog's hand as the head flipped over— and flew out of the circle.

Bog stared at the distant weapon openmouthed. He did not understand what had happened. Sos got to his feet and hefted his rope—but he still wasn't sure he could make the giant concede defeat.

Bog started to go after his club, but halted as he realized that he could not leave the circle without being adjudged the loser. He was baffled.

"Draw!" Sos shouted in a fit of inspiration. "Tie! Food! Quit!"

"Okay!" Bog replied automatically. Then, before the man could figure out what it meant, Sos took his arm in a friendly grasp and guided him out of the arena.

"It was a draw," Sos told him. "As with Sol. That means nobody won, nobody lost. We're even. So we have to fight together next time. A team."

Bog thought about it. He grinned. "Okay!" He was nothing if not agreeable, once the logic was properly presented.

That night no women happened to be available for a bracelet. Bog looked around the cabin, circled the center column once in perplexity, and finally turned on the television. For the rest of the evening he was absorbed by the silent figures gesticulating there, smiling with pleasure at the occasional cartoons. He was the first person Sos had seen actually watch television for any length of time.

Two days later they found the large Pit tribe. Twin spokesmen came out to meet them. Sos's suspicions had been correct: the master would not even talk to him.

"Very well. I challenge the master to combat in the circle."

"You," the left spokesman said dryly, "and who else?"

"And Bog the club, here."

"As you wish. You will meet one of our lesser teams first!"

"One, two, three a'time!" Bog exclaimed. "Good, good!"

"What my partner means," Sos said smoothly, "is that we will meet your first, second and third teams—consecutively." He put a handsome sneer into his voice. "Then we will sell them back to your master for suitable information. They will not be able to travel, in their condition."

"We shall see," the man said coolly.

The Pit's first team was a pair of swords. The two men were of even height and build, perhaps brothers, and seemed to know each other's location and posture without looking. This was a highly polished team that had fought together for many years, he was sure. A highly dangerous team, better than any he had trained in the badlands camp . . . and he and Bog had never fought together before. As a matter of fact, neither of them had fought in any team before, and Bog hardly understood what it was all about.

But Sos was counting on the fact that the rope weapon would be strange to these men—and Bog was Bog. "Now remember," Sos cautioned him, "I'm on *your* side. Don't hit me."

"Okay!" Bog agreed, a little dubiously. To him, anything in the circle with him was fair game, and he still wasn't entirely clear on the details of this special arrangement.

The two sworders functioned beautifully. Both were expert. While one slashed, the other parried, and while the first recovered, his partner took the offense. Every so often with no apparent signal they lunged together, twin blades swinging with synchronized precision just inches apart.

This, at any rate, was the way it was during the brief practice they engaged in prior to the formal battle. The situation changed somewhat when Bog and Sos took the circle against them.

Bog, turned on by the circle in the usual fashion, blasted away at both opponents simultaneously, while Sos stood back and twirled the end of his rope and watched, only cautioning his partner when Bog began to forget who was on which side.

The devastating club knocked both swords aside, then swept back to knock them again, to the consternation of the Pit team. They didn't know what to make of it and couldn't quite believe that it was happening.

But they were neither cowardly nor stupid. Very soon they split apart, one attempting to engage Bog defensively from the front while the other edged to the side for an angled cut.

That was when Sos's rope snaked out and caught his wrist. It was the only move Sos made, but it sufficed. Bog smashed them out of opposite sides of the circle, and Sos was right: they were not in fit condition to travel.

The second team consisted of two clubs. A good idea, Sos thought, giving the Pit director due credit, but not good enough. Bog mowed them both down zestfully while Sos continued to stay out of harm's way. The contest was over even more quickly than the first.

The Pit strategist, however, learned from experience. The third team consisted of a staffer and a netter.

Sos knew immediately that it meant trouble. He had only learned of the existence of non-standard weapons after returning to gain the advice of his mentor, Principal Jones. The very fact that a man had a net and knew how to use it in the circle meant that he had had crazy training—and that was dangerous.

It was. The moment the four were in the circle, the netter made his cast—and Bog was hopelessly entangled. He tried to swing, but the pliant nylon strands held him in. He tried to punch the net away, but did not know how. Meanwhile the netter drew the fine but exceedingly strong mesh closer and closer about him, until Bog tripped and crashed to the ground, a giant cocoon.

All this time Sos was trying savagely to reach and help his partner—but the staff held him at bay. The man made no aggressive moves; he only blocked Sos off, and at that simple task he was most effective. The staffer never looked behind him, having full confidence in his partner, and as long as he concentrated on Sos and refused to be drawn out, Sos could not hurt him.

The netter finished his job of wrapping and began rolling the hapless Bog out of the circle, net and all. Sos could guess what was coming next: the netter deprived of his own weapon, would grab for the rope, taking whatever punishment he had to to get a grip on it. Then he would keep pulling while his partner took the offensive. All the netter needed was an opening, with the staffer's distractions and two men against one. The netter would naturally be good with his bare hands on anything flexible.

"Roll, Bog, roll!" Sos shouted. "Back in the circle! Roll!

For once in his life Bog understood immediately. His wrapped body flexed like a huge grub, then countered the netter's efforts to manipulate him over the rim. Bog was hefty hunk of man and could hardly be moved against his will. Bog grunted, the staffer looked—and that was his mistake.

Sos's rope whipped around the man's neck and brought him down choking, while the Pit spectators groaned. Sos hurdled his hunching body and landed on the back of the straining netter. He clasped the man in his arms, picked him up and threw him down on top of his rising partner. A quick series of loops, and both men were bound together, the staff crosswise between them.

Sos did not foolishly approach them again. They could still maneuver together, or grab him and hang on. Instead he bent to the net, searching out the convolutions and ripping them away from Bog's body. "Lie still!" he yelled in Bog's ear as the cocoon continued to struggle. "It's me! Sos!"

Untended, the two Pit men rapidly fought free. Now they had possession of both staff and rope, while only Bog's legs were loose from the complicated, tenacious net. Sos had lost his play for time.

"Roll, Bog, roll!" he shouted again, and gave his partner a vigorous urge in the right direction. Bog kicked his legs and tried, but the motion was clumsy. The two opponents hurdled him easily—and were caught at waist height by Sos's flying tackle.

All four men landed in a heap, entangled by rope and net. But the net was spoken for while the rope was loose. Sos quickly wrapped it around all three men and knotted it securely about the striving bundle. Bog, finding the netter similarly bound, grinned through the mesh and heaved his bulk about, trying to crush the man.

Sos extracted the staff and aimed its blunt tip at the head of its owner. "Stop!" the Pit spokesman cried. "We yield! We yield!"

Sos smiled. He had not really intended to deliver such an unfair blow.

"Tomorrow the Pits will speak with you," the spokesman said, no longer so distant. He watched the three men work their way out of the involuntary embrace. "Our hospitality, tonight."

It was good hospitality. After a full meal, Sos and Bog retired to the nearest hostel, that the Pit tribe had vacated for their use. Two pretty girls showed up to claim their bracelets. "Not for me," Sos said, thinking of Sola. "No offense."

"I take both!" Bog cried. Sos left him to his pleasures; it was the rope's turn to watch television.

In the morning Sos learned why the Pits were so secretive about their persons—and why they had formed the doubles tribe. They were Siamese twins: two men joined together by a supple band of flesh at the waist. Both were swords, and Sos was certain that their teamwork, when they fought, was unexcelled.

"Yes, we know of Sol's tribe," the left one said. "Tribes, rather. Two months ago he split his group into ten subtribes of a hundred warriors each, and they are roving about the country, expanding again. One of them is coming to meet us in the circle soon."

"Oh? Who governs it?"

"Tor the Sword. He is reputed to be an able leader."

"So I can believe."

"May we inquire your business with Sol? If you seek to join a tribe yourself, we can offer you and your partner an advantageous situation—"

Sos politely declined. "My business is of a private nature. But I am sure Bog will be happy to remain for a few days by himself to give your teams practice, so long as your men, women and food hold out . . ."

12

"I S THIS THE TRIBE OF SOL OF ALL WEAPONS?" SOS INQUIRED. HE had not waited for the arrival of Tor's subordinate at the Pit camp, much as he would have enjoyed being on hand for the contest of wits between Tor and the perceptive Pit strategist. It would probably be a standoff. It was Sol he was after, and now that he knew where to find him no further delay was tolerable.

As it happened, he had met Tor on the way, and obtained updating and redirection—but it was hard to believe, even so, that this was the proper camp.

Warriors were practicing everywhere, none of them familiar. Yet this was the only major group in the arena, so the directions had not been mistaken. Had he traveled a month only to encounter Sol's conqueror? He hoped not. The camp was well disciplined, but he did not like its atmosphere.

"Speak to Vit the Sword," the nearest man told him.

Sos searched out the main tent and asked for Vit. "Who are you?" the tent guard, a swarthy dagger, demanded, eying the bird on his shoulder.

"Step into the circle and I will show you who I am!" Sos said angrily. He had had enough of such bureaucracy.

The guard whistled and a man detached himself from practice and trotted over. "This intruder wishes to make himself known in the circle," the dagger said contemptuously. "Oblige him."

The man turned to study Sos.

"Mok the Morningstar!" Sos cried.

Mok started. "Sos! You have come back—and Stupid, too! I did not recognize you, in all that muscle!"

"You know this man?" the guard inquired.

"Know him! This is Sos—the man who built this tribe! Sol's friend!"

The guard shrugged indifferently. "Let him prove it in the circle."

"You nuts? He doesn't carry a—" Mok paused. "Or *do* you, now?"

Sos had his rope about him, but the man had not recognized it as a weapon. "I do. Come, I'll demonstrate."

"Why not try it against the staff or sticks?" Mok suggested diplomatically. "My weapon is—"

"Is dangerous? You seem to lack faith in my prowess."

"Oh, no," Mok protested, obviously insincere. "But you know how it is with the star. One accident—"

Sos laughed. "You force me to vindicate myself. Come—I'll make a believer out of you."

Mok accompanied him to the circle, ill at ease. "If anything happens—"

"This is my weapon," Sos said, hefting a coil of rope. "If you are afraid to face it, summon a better man."

Several neighboring men chuckled, and Mok had to take the circle. Sos knew the jibe had been unfair; the man had wanted to spare him from possible mutilation. Mok was no coward, and since he was still with the tribe, his skill was sufficient too. But it was important that the rope prove itself as a real weapon; men like Mok would not believe in Sos's new status as a warrior otherwise.

Friendship ended in the circle, always. Mok lifted his morningstar and whirled the spiked ball in an overhead spiral. He had to attack, since the weapon could not be used defensively. Sos had never faced the star before and discovered that it was a peculiarly frightening experience. Even the faint tune of air passing the circling spikes was ominous.

Sos backed away, treating the flying ball with utmost respect. He fired a length of rope at it, caught the metal chain, fouled it, and yanked ball, chain and handle out of Mok's hand. Mok stood there staring, as Bog had done before him. The spectators laughed.

"If any of you think you can do better, step inside," Sos invited.

A sticker was quick to accept the challenge—and as quick to fall to the throttle-loop. This time it was Mok who laughed. "Come—you must see Vit now!"

A group of men continued to stand around the vacated circle, murmuring as Sos left. They had never witnessed such a performance.

"I'm glad you're back," Mok confided as they came to the tent. "Things aren't the same around here since—" he broke off as they approached the guard.

This time there was no trouble about entry. Mok ushered him into the leader's presence.

"Yes?" Vit was a tall slender, dour man of middle years who looked familiar. The name, also, jogged an image. Then Sos placed him: the sworder that Dal the Dagger had humiliated, back in the first full-fledged tribal encounter. Times had certainly changed!

"I am Sos the rope. I have come to talk to Sol."

"By what right?"

Mok started to explain, but Sos had had enough. He knew Vit recognized him and was simply placing difficulties in his way. "By the right of my weapon! Challenge me in the circle before you attempt to balk me!" It was good to be able to assume this posture again; the weapon made all the difference. Sos realized that he was being less than reasonable, and enjoyed the feeling.

Vit merely looked at him. "Are you that rope who disarmed Bog the club, five weeks ago in the east?"

"I am." Sos was beginning to appreciate why Vit had risen to such a position of power so rapidly: he had complete command of his temper and knew his business. Apparently supremacy in the circle was no longer a requirement for leadership.

"Sol will see you tomorrow."

"Tomorrow!"

"He is absent on business today. Accept our hospitality tonight."

Sol away on business? He did not like the smell of that. Sol should have no reason to recruit warriors alone, any more—not with ten tribes to manage, the nucleus of his empire. He could not be inspecting any of those tribes, either; the nearest was at least a week away.

A woman emerged from a compartment and walked slowly toward them. She was dressed in a breathtakingly snug sarong and wore very long, very black hair.

It was Sola.

Sos started toward her, only to be blocked by Vit. "Eyes off that woman! She belongs to the master!"

Sola looked up and recognized him. "Sos!" she cried then checked herself. "I know this man," she said formally to Vit. "I will speak to him."

"You will *not* speak to him." Vit stood firmly between them.

Sos gripped his rope, furious, but Sola backed away and retreated into her compartment. Mok tugged his arm, and he controlled himself and wheeled about. Something was certainly wrong, but this

was not the moment for action. It would not be wise to betray his former intimacy with Sola.

"All the old stalwarts are gone," Mok said sadly as they emerged. "Tyl, Tor, Sav, Tun—hardly any of the ones we built the badlands camp with are here today."

"What happened to them?" He knew already, but wanted more information. The more he saw of this tribe, the less he liked it. *Was* Sol still in control, or had he become a figurehead? Had there been some private treachery to incapacitate him?

"They command the other tribes. Sol trusts no one you did not train. We need you again, Sos. I wish we were back in the badlands, the way it was before."

"Sol seems to trust Vit."

"Not to command. This is Sol's own tribe, and he runs it himself, with advisors. Vit just handles the details."

"Such as keeping Sola penned up?"

"Sol makes him do it. She is allowed to see no one while he is away. Sol would kill Vit if—but I told you, everything is different."

Sos agreed, profoundly disturbed. The camp was efficient, but the men were strangers to him. He recognized no more than half a dozen of the hundred or so he saw. It was a strange pass when the closest companion he could find in Sol's tribe was Mok—whose dealing with him had always been brief before. This was not, in fact, a tribe at all; it was a military camp, of the type he had read about, with a military martinet in charge. The *esprit de corps* he had fostered was gone.

He accepted a small tent on the outskirts, alone, for the night. He was troubled, but still did not want to act until he understood the ramifications of what he had observed. Evidently the dour Vit had been put in charge because he followed orders without imagination and was probably completely trustworthy in that respect. But why the need? Something had gone drastically wrong, and he could not believe that his own absence could account for it. Tor's tribe was hardly like this. What had taken the spirit out of Sol's drive for empire?

A woman came quietly to the tent. "Bracelet?" she inquired, her voice muffled, her face hidden in the dusk.

"No!" he snapped, turning his eyes from the hourglass figure that showed in provocative silhouette against the distant evening fires.

She tugged open the mesh and kneeled to show her face. "Would you shame me, Sos?"

"I asked for no woman," he said, not looking at her.

"Go away. No offense."

She did not move. "Greensleeves," she murmured.

His head jerked up. "Sola!"

"It was never your habit to make me wait so long for recognition," she said with wry reproof. "Let me in before someone sees." She scrambled inside and refastened the mesh. "I changed places with the girl assigned, so I think we're safe. But still—"

"What are you doing here? I thought you weren't—"

She stripped and crawled into his bedroll. "You must have been exercising!"

"Not any more."

"Oh, but you have! I never felt such a muscular body."

"I mean we're not—lovers any more. If you won't meet me by day, I won't meet you by night."

"Why did you come, then?" she inquired, placing against him a body that had become magnificent. Her pregnancy of the year before had enhanced her physical attributes.

"I came to claim you honorably."

"Claim me, then! No man but you has touched me since we first met."

"Tomorrow. Give back his bracelet and take mine, publicly."

"I will," she said. "Now—"

"No!"

She drew back and tried to see his face in the dark. "You mean it."

"I love you. I came for you. But I will have you honorably."

She sighed. "Honor is not quite—that simple, Sos." But she got up and began putting on her clothing.

"What has happened here? Where is Sol? Why are you hiding from people?"

"You left us, Sos. That's what happened. You were the heart of us."

"That doesn't make sense. I had to leave. You were having the baby. *His* son."

"No."

"That was the price of you. I will not pay it again. This time it has to be my son, conceived upon my bracelet."

"You don't understand *anything*!" she cried in frustration.

He paused, knowing the mystery to be yet unfathomed. "Did it die?"

"No! That's not the point. That—oh, you stupid, stupid clubhead! You—" She choked over her own emotion and faced away from him, sobbing.

She was more artful, too, than she had been, he thought. He did not yield. He let her run down, unmoving.

Finally she wiped her face and crawled out of the tent. He was alone.

13

OL WAS A LITTLE LEANER, A LITTLE MORE SERIOUS, BUT retained the uncanny grace his coordination provided. "You came!" he exclaimed, grasping Sos's hand in an unusual display of pleasure.

"Yesterday," Sos said, somewhat embarrassed. "I saw Vit, but he wouldn't let me talk to your wife, and I hardly know the others here." How much should he say?

"She should have come to you anyway. Vit knows nothing." He paused reflectively. "We do not get along. She keeps to herself."

So Sol still didn't care about Sola. He had protected her for the sake of the coming heir and no longer even bothered with pretense. But why, then, had he kept her isolated? It had never been Sol's way to be pointlessly selfish.

"I have a weapon now," Sos said. Then, as the other looked at him: "The rope."

"I am glad of it."

There did not seem to be much else to say. Their reunion, like their parting, was an awkward thing.

"Come," Sol said abruptly. "I will show her to you."

Sos followed him into the main tent, uncomfortably off-balance. He should have admitted that he *had* talked with Sola and prevented this spurious introduction. He had come on a matter of honor, yet he was making himself a liar.

Nothing was falling out quite the way he had expected—but the differences were intangible. The subtle wrongnesses were entangling him, as though he had fallen prey in the circle to the net.

They stopped before a homemade crib in a small compartment. Sol leaned down to pick up a chuckling baby. "This is my daughter," he said. "Six months, this week."

Sos stood with one hand on his rope, speechless gazing at the black-haired infant. A daughter! Somehow that possibility had never occurred to him.

"She will be as beautiful as her mother," Sol said proudly. "See her smile."

"Yes," Sos agreed, feeling every bit as stupid as Sola had called him. The name should not have gone to his bird.

"Come," Sol repeated. "We will take her for a walk." He hefted the baby upon his shoulder and led the way. Sos followed numbly, realizing that *this* was the female they had come to see, not the mother. If he had only known, or guessed, or allowed himself to hear, last night. . . .

Sola met them at the entrance. "I would come," she said

Sol sounded annoyed. "Come, then, woman. We only walk."

The little party threaded its way out of the camp and into the nearby forest. It was like old times, when they had journeyed to the badlands—yet completely different. What incredible things had grown from the early coincidence of names!

This was all wrong. He had come to claim the woman he loved, to challenge Sol for her in the circle if he had to, yet he could not get the words out. He loved her and she loved him and her nominal husband admitted the marriage was futile—but Sos felt like a terrible intruder.

Stupid flew ahead, happy to sport among the forest shadows; or perhaps there were insects there.

This could not go on. "I came for Sola," he said baldly.

Sol did not even hesitate. "Take her." It was as though the woman were not present.

"My bracelet, on her wrist," Sos said, wondering whether he had been understood. "My children by her. She shall be Sosa."

"Certainly."

This was beyond credence. "You have no conditions?"

"Only your friendship."

Sos sputtered, "This is not a friendly matter!"

"Why not? I have preserved her only for you."

"You—Vit—?" This elaborate guardianship had been for his, Sos's benefit? "Why—?"

"I would have her take no lesser name," Sol said.

Why not, indeed? There seemed to be no barrier to an amicable changeover but it was wrong. It couldn't work. He could not put his finger on the flaw, but knew there was something.

"Give me Soli," Sola said.

Sol handed the baby over. She opened her dress and held Soli to her breast to nurse as they walked.

And that was it. The baby! "Can she leave her mother?" Sos asked.

"No," Sola replied.

"You will not take my daughter," Sol said, raising his voice for the first time.

"No—of course not. But until she is weaned—"

"Until, nothing," Sola said firmly. "She's *my* daughter, too. She stays with me."

"Soli is mine!" Sol said with utter conviction. "You woman—stay or go as you will, wear whose clasp you will—but Soli is mine."

The baby looked up and began to cry. Sol reached over and took the little girl, and she fell contentedly silent. Sola made a face but said nothing.

"I make no claim upon your daughter," Sos said carefully. "But if she cannot leave her mother—"

Sol found a fallen tree and sat down upon it, balancing Soli upon his knee. "Sorrow fell upon our camp when you departed. Now you are back, and with your weapon. Govern my tribe, my empire, as you did before. I would have you by my side again."

"But I came to take Sola away with me! She cannot stay here after she exchanges bracelets. It would bring shame upon us both."

"Why?"

"Sosa nursing Sol's child?"

Sol thought about it. "Let her wear my bracelet, then. She will still be yours."

"You would wear the horns?"

Sol jiggled Soli on his knee. He began to hum a tune: then, catching the range, he sang the words in a fine, clear tenor:

From this valley they say you are going
We shall miss your bright eyes and
*   sweet smile*
For they say you are taking the
*   sunshine*
That brightens our pathway a while.

Come and sit by my—

Sos interrupted him, appalled. "You heard!"

"I heard who my true friend was, when I was in fever and could not move my body or save myself from injury. I heard who carried me when I would have died. If I must wear the horns, these are the horns I would wear, for all to see."

"No!" Sos cried, shocked.

"Only leave me my daughter; the rest is yours."

"Not dishonor!" Yet it seemed late for this protest. "I will not accept dishonor—yours or mine."

"Nor I," Sola said quietly. "Not now."

"How can there be dishonor among us!" Sol said fervently. "There is only friendship."

They faced each other in silence then, searching for the solution. Sos ran over the alternatives in his mind, again and again, but nothing changed. He could leave—and give up all his dreams of union with the woman he loved, while she remained with a man she did *not* love and who cared nothing for her. Could he take comfort in such as blonde Miss Smith, while that situation existed? Or he could stay—and accept the dishonorable liaison that would surely emerge, knowing himself to be unworthy of his position and his weapon.

Or he could fight—for a woman *and* honor. Everything or nothing.

Sol met his gaze. He had come to the same conclusion.

"Make a circle," he said.

"No!" Sola cried, realizing what was happening. "It is wrong either way!"

"That is why it must be settled in the circle," Sos told her regretfully. "You and your daughter must be together. You *shall* be—either way."

"I will leave Soli," she said with difficulty. "Do not fight again."

Sol still sat holding the baby, looking very little like the master of an empire. "No—for a mother to leave her child is worse than for the leader to leave his tribe. I did not think of that before, but I know it now."

"But you brought no weapon," she said, trying to stave it off.

Sol ignored her and looked at Sos. "I would not kill you. You may serve me if you wish, and do what you wish—but never again will you bear weapon against me," he finished with some force.

"I would not kill you either. You may keep your weapons and your empire—but child and mother go with me."

And that defined it. If Sol won, Sos would be deprived of any honorable means to advance his case, which would mean that he was helpless. If Sos won, Sol would have to give up the baby, leaving Sola free to go with the rope.

The winner would have his desire; the loser, what remained.

What remained, despite the theoretical generosity of the terms, was the mountain. Sos would not remain to adulterate the bracelet Sola wore or return in shame to the crazies' establishment. Sol would spurn his empire, once mastered in combat; that had always been clear. It was not a pretty situation, and the victor would have his sorrows, but it was a fair solution. Trial by combat.

"Make the circle," Sol said again.

"But your weapon—" They were repeating themselves. Neither really wanted to fight. Was there some other way out?

Sol handed the baby to Sola and peered through the trees. He located a suitable sapling and stripped the branches and leaves by hand. Seeing his intent, Sos proceeded to clear a place on the forest floor to form a roughly level disk of earth the proper size. The arrangements were crude, but this was not a matter either man cared to advertise in front of the tribe.

They met, standing on opposite sides of the makeshift arena, Sola standing anxiously near. The scene reminded Sos of their first encounter, except for the baby in Sola's arms.

Sos now far outweighed his opponent, and held a weapon he was sure Sol had never seen before. Sol, on the other hand, held a makeshift implement, but he was the finest warrior ever seen in the area, and the weapon he had fashioned was a staff.

The one thing the rope was weak against.

Had Sol's barrow been available, he might have taken the sword or the club or one of the other standardized instruments of battle, but in his self-reliance he had procured what could be had from nature, and with it, though he could not know it yet, the victory.

"After this we shall be friends," Sol said.

"We shall be friends." And somehow that was more important than all the rest of it.

They stepped into the circle.

The baby cried.

14

IT WAS MIDSUMMER BY THE TIME HE STOOD AT THE FOOT OF THE mountain. This was a strange heap of lava and slag towering above the twisted landscape, sculptured in some manner by the Blast but free of radiation. Shrubs and stunted trees approached the base, but only weeds and lichen ascended the mountain itself.

Sos peered up but could not see the top. A few hundred yards ahead, great projections of metallic material obscured the view, asymmetrical and ugly. Gliding birds of prey circled high in the haze overhead, watching him.

There was wind upon the mountain, not fierce, but howling dismally around the brutal serrations. The sky above it was overcast and yellowish.

This was surely the mountain of death. No one could mistake it.

He touched his fingers to his shoulder and lifted Stupid. The bird had never been handsome; his mottled brown feathers always seemed to have been recently ruffled, and the distribution of colors remained haphazard—but Sos had become accustomed to every avian mannerism in the time they had had their association. "This is about as far as you go, little friend," he said. "I go up, never to come down again—but it is not your turn. Those vultures aren't after *you*."

He flicked the bird into the air, but Stupid spread his wings, circled, and came to roost again upon his shoulder.

Sos shrugged. "I give you your freedom, but you do not take it. Stupid." It was meaningless, but he was touched. How could the bird know what was ahead?

For that matter, how could anyone know? How much of human loyalty and love was simply ignorance of destiny?

He still wore the rope, but no longer as a weapon. He caught a languishing sapling and stripped it as Sol had done, making himself a crude staff for balance

during the climb. He adjusted his heavy pack and moved out.

The projections *were* metal—enormous sheets and beams melted at the edges and corners, securely embedded in the main mass, the crevices filled with pebbles and dirt. It was as though a thousand men had shoved it together and set fire to it all—assuming that metal would burn. Perhaps they had poured alcohol upon it? Of course not; this was the handiwork of the Blast.

Even at this terminal stage of his life, Sos retained his curiosity about the phenomenon of the Blast. What was its nature, and how had it wrought such diverse things as the invisibly dangerous badlands and the mountain of death? If it had been unleashed somehow by man himself, as the crazies claimed, why had the ancients chosen to do it?

It was the riddle of all things, unanswerable as ever. The modern world began with the Blast; what preceded it was largely conjecture. The crazies claimed that there had been a strange other society before it, a world of incredible machines and luxury and knowledge, little of which survived.

But while he half believed them, and the venerable texts made convincing evidence, the practical side of him set it all aside as unproven. He had described past history to others as though it were fact, but it was as realistic to believe that the books themselves, along with the men and landscape, had been created in one moment from the void, by the Blast.

He was delaying the climb unnecessarily. If he meant to do it, now was the time. If fear turned him back, he should admit it, rather than pretending to philosophize. One way or the other: action.

He roped a beam and hauled himself up, staff jammed down between his back and the pack. There was probably an easier way to ascend, since the many men who had gone before him would not have had ropes or known how to use them, but he had not come to expire the easy way. Stupid, dislodged, flew up and perched on the beam, peeking down at him. The bird never criticized, never got in the way; he winged himself to safety when there was action in the circle or in the tent at night, but always came back. He waited only for the conquest of this particular hazard, before rejoining his companion. Was this the definition of true friendship?

Sos scrambled to the upper surface of the beam and dislodged the rope. Sure enough, Stupid swooped in, brushing the tip of a wing against his right ear. Always the right shoulder, never the left! But not for long—the outcropping was merely the first of many, vertical and horizontal and angled, large and small and indefinite, straight and looped and twisted. It would be a tedious, grueling climb.

As evening came, he unlimbered warmer clothing from the pack and ate the solid bread he had found stocked for the mountaineers at the nearest cabin. How considerate of the crazies, to make available the stuff of life for those bent on dying!

He had looked at everything in that hostel, knowing that he would not have another chance . . . even the television. It was the same silent meaningless pantomime as ever; men and women garbed like exaggerated crazies, fighting and kissing in brazen openness but never using proper weapons or making proper love. It was possible, with concentration, to make out portions of some kind of story—but every time it seemed to be making sense the scene would change and different characters would appear holding up glasses of liquid that foamed or putting slender cylinders in their mouths and burning them. No wonder no one watched it! He had once asked Jones about the television, but the principal had only smiled and said that the maintenance of that type of technology was not in his department. It was all broadcast from pre-Blast tapes, anyway, Jones explained.

Sos put such foolishness aside. There were practical problems to be considered. He had loaded the pack carefully, knowing that a man could starve anywhere if he ventured without adequate preparation. The mountain was a special demise, not to be demeaned by common hunger or thirst. He had already consumed the quart bottle of fortified water, knowing that there would be edible snow at the height to take its place. Whatever lurked, it was not malnutrition.

What *did* lurk? No one had been able to tell him, since it was a one-way journey, and the books were strangely reticent. The books all seemed to stop just *before* the Blast; only scattered manuals used by the crazies were dated after it. That could be a sign that the books were pre-Blast—or it could discredit them entirely, since not one of them related to the *real* world. They and the television were parts of the elaborate and mystifying myth-world framework whose existence he believed one day and denied the next. The mountain could be yet another aspect of it.

Well, since he couldn't turn his mind off, there was a very practical way to find out. He would mount the mountain and

see for himself. Death, at least, could not be secondhand.

Stupid fluttered about, searching out flying insects, but there did not seem to be many. "Go back down, birdbrain." Sos advised him. "This is no place for you." It seemed that the bird obeyed, for he disappeared from sight, and Sos yielded himself to the turbulence of semi-consciousness: television and iron beams and Sola's somber face and nebulous uncertainties about the nature of the extinction he sought. But in the cold morning Stupid was back, as Sos had known he would be.

The second day of the climb was easier than the first, and he covered three times the distance. The tangled metal gave way to packed rubble clogged by weeds: huge sections of dissolving rubber in the shape of a torus, oblong sheets of metal a few inches long, sections of ancient boots, baked clay fragments, plastic cups and hundreds of bronze and silver coins. These were the artifacts of pre-Blast civilization, according to the books; he could not imagine what the monstrous rubber doughnuts were for, but the rest appeared to be implements similar to those stocked in the hostels. The coins were supposed to have been symbols of status; to possess many of them had been like victory in the circle.

If the books could be believed.

Late in the afternoon, it rained. Sos dug one of the cups out of the ground, knocked out the caked dirt and held it up to trap the water. He was thirsty, and the snow was farther away than he had expected. Stupid sat hunched on his shoulder, hating the drenching; Sos finally propped up a flap of the pack to shield the little bird.

But in the evening there were more insects abroad, as though the soaking had forced them out, and that was good. He applied repellant against the mosquitoes while Stupid zoomed vigorously, making up for lean times.

Sos had kept his mind on his task, but now that the mountain had lost its novelty his thoughts returned to the most emotional episodes of his life. He remembered the first meeting with Sol, both of them comparatively new to the circle, still exploring the world and feeling their way cautiously in protocol and battle. Evidently Sol had tried all his weapons out in sport encounters until sure of himself; then, with their evening's discussion, that first night, Sol had seen the possible mechanisms of advancement. Play had stopped for them both, that day and night, and already their feet had been treading out the destinies leading to power for the one, and for the other—the mountain.

He remembered Sola, then an innocent girl, lovely and anxious to prove herself by the bracelet. She had proven herself—but not by the bracelet she wore. That, more than anything else, had led him here.

Strange, that the three should meet like that. Had it been just the two men, the empire might even now be uniting them. Had the girl appeared before or after, he might have taken her for a night and gone on, never missing her. But it had been a triple union, and the male empire had been sown with the female seed of destruction even as it sprouted. It was not the particular girl who mattered, but the presence at the inception. Why had she come *then*!

He closed his eyes and saw the staff, blindingly swift, blocking him, striking

him, meeting him everywhere he turned, no instrument of defense but savage offense; the length of it across his body, the end of it flying at his face, fouling his rope, outmaneuvering him, beating down his offense and his defense. . . .

And now the mountain, the only honorable alternative. He had lost to the better man.

He slept, knowing that even victory would not have been the solution. He had been in the wrong—not totally, but wrong on balance.

On the third day the snows began. He wrapped the last of the protective clothing around him and kept moving. Stupid clung to him, seemingly not too uncomfortable. Sos scooped up handfuls of the white powder and crammed them into his mouth for water, though the stuff numbed his cheeks and tongue and melted grudgingly down into almost nothing. By nightfall he was ploughing through drifts several inches deep and had to step carefully to avoid treacherous pitfalls that did not show in the leveled surface.

There was no shelter. He lay on his side, facing away from the wind, comfortable enough in the protective wrappings. Stupid settled down beside his face, shivering, and suddenly he realized that the bird had no way to forage anymore. Not in the snow. There would be no living insects here.

He dug a handful of bread out of the pack and held a crumb to Stupid's beak; but there was no response. "You'll starve," he said with concern, but did not know what to do about it. He saw the feathers shaking, and finally took off his left glove, cupped the bird in his bare warm palm, and held his gloved right hand to the back of the exposed one. He would have to make sure he didn't roll or move his hands while sleeping, or he would crush the fragile body.

He woke several times in the night as gusts of cold snow slapped his face and pried into his collar, but his left hand never moved. He felt the bird shivering from time to time and cupped it close to his chest, hoping for a suitable compromise between warmth and safety. He had too much strength and Stupid was too small; better to allow some shivering than to. . . .

Stupid seemed all right in the morning, but Sos knew this could not last. The bird was not adapted to snow; even his coloration was wrong. "Go back down," he urged. "Down. Where it is warm. Insects." He threw the tiny body into the air, downhill, but to no avail; Stupid spread his wings and struggled valiantly with the cold, harsh air, uphill, and would not leave.

Yet, Sos asked himself as he took the bird in hand again and continued climbing, was this misplaced loyalty any more foolish than Sol's determination to retain a daughter he had not sired? A *daughter*? Or Sos's own adherence to a code of honor already severely violated? Men were irrational creatures; why not birds too? If separation were so difficult, they would die together.

A storm came up that fourth day. Sos drove onward, his face numbed in the slashing wind. He had goggles, tinted to protect his eyes, and he put them on now, but the nose and mouth were still exposed. When he put his hand up he discovered a beard of ice superimposed upon his natural one. He tried to knock it off, but knew it would form again.

Stupid flew up as he stumbled and waved his hands. Sos guided the bird to his shoulder, where at least there was some stability. Another slip like that and the bird would be smashed, if he continued to carry it in his hand.

The wind stabbed into his clothing. Earlier he had been sweating, finding the wrappings cumbersome; now the moisture seemed to be caking into ice against his body. That had been a mistake; he should have governed his dress and pace so that he never perspired. There was nowhere for the moisture to go, so of course it eventually froze. He had learned this lesson too late.

This, then, was the death of the mountain. Freezing in the blizzardly upper regions or falling into some concealed crevasse . . . he had been watching the lay of the land, but already he had slipped and fallen several times, and only luck had made his errors harmless. The cold crept in through his garments, draining his visibility, and the eventual result was clear. No person had ever returned from the mountain, if the stories were true, and no bodies had ever been discovered or recovered. No wonder!

Yet this was not the kind of mountain he had heard about elsewhere. After the metal jumble near the base—how many days ago?—there had been no extreme irregularities, no jagged edges, sheer cliffs or preposterous ice bridges. He had seen no alternate ranges or major passes when the sky was clear. The side of this mountain tilted up fairly steadily, fairly safely, like that of an inverted bowl. Only the cold presented a genuine hazard.

Surely there was no impediment to those who elected to descend again. Not all, or even most, but some must have given it up and returned to the foot, either choosing a less strenuous way to die or deciding to live after all. He could still turn about himself.

He picked the quiet bird from his shoulder, disengaging the claws with difficulty. "How about it, Stupid? Have we had enough?"

There was no response. The little body was stiff.

He brought it close to his face, not wanting to believe. He spread one wing gently with his fingers, but it was rigid. Stupid had died rather than desert his companion and Sos had not even known the moment of his passing

True friendship. . . .

He laid the feathered corpse upon the snow and covered it over, a lump in his throat. "I'm sorry, little friend," he said. "I guess a man takes more dying than a bird." Nothing utterable came to mind beyond that, inadequate as it was.

He faced up the mountain and tramped ahead.

The world was a bleak place now. He had taken the bird pretty much for granted, but the sudden, silent loss was staggering. Now there was nothing he could do but go through with it. He had killed a faithful friend, and there was a raw place in his breast that would not ease.

Yet it was not the first time his folly had damaged another. All Sol had asked was friendship—and, rather than grant him that, Sos had forced him into the circle. What had been so damned urgent about his own definition honor? Why had he resisted Sol's ultimate offer with such determination? Was it because he had used a limited concept of honor to promote his own selfish objectives ruthlessly, no matter who else was sacrificed? And, failing in these, bringing further pain by wiping out whatever else might have been salvaged?

He thought again of Stupid, so recently dead upon his shoulder, and had his answer.

The mountain steepened. The storm intensified. Let it come! he thought; it was what he had come for. He could no longer tell whether it was day or night. Ice rimmed his goggles, if they were still on. He wasn't sure and didn't care. Everywhere was whirling whiteness. He was panting, his lungs were burning and he wasn't getting enough air. The steep snowscape before him went on and on; there was no end to it.

He did not realize that he had fallen until he choked on the snow. He tried to stand up, but his limbs did not respond properly. "Come *on!*" he heard Sola calling him, and he listened though he knew it for illusion. He did go on, but more securely: on hands and knees.

Then he was crawling on his belly, numb everywhere except for the heartache.

At last the pleasant lassitude obliterated even that.

15

UP MUSCLES. IT'S BETTER IF YOU WALK AROUND, GET THE system functioning again and all that."

Sos recovered unwillingly. He tried to open his eyes, but the darkness remained.

"Uh-uh! Leave that bandage alone. Even if you aren't snowblind, you're frostbit. Here, take my hand." A firm man's hand thrust itself against his arm.

"Did I die?" Sos asked, bracing against the proffered palm as he stood.

"Yes. In a manner of speaking. You will never be seen on the surface again."

"And—Stupid?"

"What?"

"My bird, Stupid. Did he come here too?"

The man paused. "Either there's a misunderstanding, or you are insolent as hell."

Sos constricted his fingers on the man's arm, bringing a exclamation of pain. He caught at the bandage on his head with his free hand and ripped it off. There was bright pain as packed gauze came away from his eyeballs, but he could see again.

He was in a hostel room, standing before a standard bunk surrounded by unstandard equipment. He wore his pantaloons but nothing else. A thin man in an effeminate white smock winced with the continuing pressure of his grip. Sos released him, looking for the exit.

Not a hostel room, for this room was square. The standard furnishings had given him the impression. He had never seen a cabin this shape, however.

"I must say, that's an unusual recovery!" the man remarked, rubbing his arm. He was of middle age with sparse hair and pale features: obviously long parted from sun and circle.

"Are you a crazy?"

"Most people in your situation are content to inquire 'Where am I?' or something mundane like that. You're certainly original."

"I did not come to the mountain to be mocked," Sos said, advancing on him.

The man touched a button in the wall. "We have a live one," he said.

"So I see," a feminine voice replied from nowhere. An intercom, Sos realized. So they *were* crazies. "Put him in the rec room. I'll handle it."

The man touched a second button. A door slid open beside him. "Straight to the end. All your questions will be answered."

Sos brushed by him, more anxious to find the way out than to question an uncooperative stranger. But the hall did not lead out; it continued interminably, closed doors on either side. This was certainly no hostel, nor was it a building like the school run by the crazies. It was too big.

He tried a door, finding it locked. He thought about breaking it down, but was afraid that would take too much time. He had a headache, his muscles were stiff and flaccid at once, his stomach queasy. He felt quite sick, physically, and just wanted to get out before any more annoying strangers came along.

The end door was open. He stepped into a very large room filled with angular structures: horizontal bars, vertical rods, enormous boxes seemingly formed of staffs tied together at right angles. He had no idea what it all signified and was too dizzy and ill to care.

A light hand fell across his arm, making him jump. He grabbed for his rope and whirled to face the enemy.

The rope was gone, of course, and the one who touched him was a girl. Her head did not even reach to his shoulder.

She wore a baggy coverall, and her hair was bound in a close-fitting headcap, making her look boyish. Her tiny feet were bare.

Sos relaxed, embarrassed, though his head still throbbed and the place still disturbed him by its confinement. He had never been this tense before, yet inadequate. If only he could get out into the open forest . . .

"Let me have this," the little girl said. Her feather-gentle fingers slid across his forearm and fastened upon the bracelet. In a moment she had it off.

He grabbed for it angrily, but she eluded him. "What are you doing?" he demanded.

She fitted the golden clasp over her own wrist and squeezed it snug. "Very nice. I always wanted one of these," she said pertly. She lifted a pixie eyebrow at him. "What's your name?"

"Sos the—Sos," he said, remembering his defeat in the circle and considering himself, therefore, weaponless. He reached for her again, but she danced nimbly away. "I did not give that to you!"

"Take it back, then," she said, holding out her wrist. Her arm was slender but aesthetically rounded, and he wondered just how young she was. Certainly not old enough to be playing such games with a grown man.

Once more he reached . . . and grasped air. "Girl, you anger me."

"If you are as slow to anger as you are to move, I have nothing to worry about, monster."

This time he leaped for her, slow neither to anger nor to motion—and missed her again.

"Come on, baby," she cooed, wriggling her upraised wrist so that the metal band glittered enticingly. "You don't like being mocked, you say, so don't let a woman get away with anything. Catch me."

He saw that she wanted him to chase her, and knew that he should not oblige; but the pain in his head and body cut short his caution and substituted naked fury. He ran after her.

She skipped fleetly beside the wall, looking back at him and giggling. She was so small and light that agility was natural to her; her body could not have weighed more than a hundred pounds including the shapeless garment. As he gained on her, she dodged to the side and swung around a vertical bar, making him stumble cumbersomely.

"Lucky you aren't in the cir-cle!" she trilled. "You can't even keep your feet!"

By the time he got on her trail once more, she was in among the poles, weaving around them with a facility obviously stemming from long experience.

Sos followed, grasping the uprights and swinging his body past them with increasing dexterity. Now that he was exerting himself he felt better, as though he were throwing off the lethargy of the freezing mountains. Again he gained—and again she surprised him.

She leaped into the air and caught the bottom rung of a ladder suspended from the high ceiling. She flipped athletically and hooked it with her feet, then ascended as though she had no weight at all. In moments she was far out of reach.

Sos took hold of the lowest rung, just within his range, and discovered that it was made of flexible plastic, as were the two vertical columns. He jerked experimentally. A ripple ran up the ropes, jarring the girl. Ropes? He smiled and shook harder, forcing her to cling tightly in order not to be shaken off. Then, certain he had her trapped, he gradually hauled down until his entire weight was suspended.

It would hold him. He hoisted himself to the rung, unused to this type of exercise but able to adapt. He could handle a rope.

She peeked down, alarmed, but he climbed steadily, watching her. In a few seconds he knew he would be able to grab her foot and haul her down with him.

She threaded her legs through the top of the ladder and leaned out upside down, twisting her body and touching it with her freed hands. The coverall came away from her shoulders and to her hips—up or down, depending upon perspective—then she caught one arm in the ladder and stripped herself the rest of the way. She wore a slight, snug two-piece suit underneath that decorated little more than her bosom and buttocks. Sos revised his estimate of her age sharply upward; she was as well rounded a woman as he had seen.

She contemplated him with that elfin expression, spread out the coveralls, and dropped them neatly upon his raised face.

He cursed and pawed it away, almost losing his grip on the ladder. She was shaking it now, perhaps in belief she could dislodge him while he was blinded, and he felt her strike his clutching hand.

By the time he had secured his position and cast off the clinging, faintly scented cloth, she was standing on the floor below him, giggling merrily. She had gone right by him!

"Don't you want your bracelet, clumsy?" she teased.

Sos handed himself down and dropped to the floor, but she was gone again. This time she mounted the boxlike structure, wriggling over and under the bars as though she were a flying snake. He ran to the base, but she was amidst it all and he could not get at her from any direction without climbing into it himself. He knew by this time that he could never catch her that way; she was a gymnast whose size and weight made her entirely at home here.

"All right," he said, disgruntled but no longer angry. He took the time to admire her lithe and healthy body. Who would have suspected such rondure in so brief a package? "Keep it."

A moment and several gyrations and she stood beside him. "Give up?"

He snapped his fingers over her upper arm, using the trick of his rope throw to make the motion too quick to elude. "No."

She did not even wince at the cruel pressure. She sliced her free hand sidewise into his stomach, just below the rib cage and angling up, fingers flat and stiff.

He was astonished at the force of the blow, coming as it did with so little warning, and he was momentarily paralyzed. Still, he maintained his grip and tightened it until her firm young flesh was crushed against the bone.

Even so, she did not shrink or exclaim. She struck him again with that peculiar flat of the hand, this time across the throat. Incredible agony blossomed there. His stomach drove its content up into his mouth and he could not even catch his breath or cry out. He let go, gagging and choking.

When he became aware of his surroundings again he was sitting on the floor and she was kneeling astride his legs and resting her hands upon his shoulders. "I'm sorry I did that, Sos. But you are very strong."

He stared dully at her, realizing that she was somewhat more talented than he had guessed. She was a woman, but her blows had been sure.

"I really *would* like to keep your bracelet, Sos. I know what it means."

He thought about the way Sol had given his bracelet to Sola. The initial carelessness of the act had not signified any corresponding laxity in the relationship, though its terms were strange. Was he now to present his own bracelet even more capriciously, simply because a woman asked for it? He tried to speak, but his larynx, still constricted from the knock, did not permit it.

She held out her wrist to him and did not retreat. He reached up slowly and circled it with his fingers. He remembered that he had fought for Sola and lost, while this woman had, in more than a manner of speaking, challenged him for the bracelet and won.

Perhaps it had to be taken from him. Had he been ready to give it away, he should have given it to blonde Miss Smith, knowing that she wanted it. Sola, too, had forced her love upon him and made him respond. He did not like what this seemed to indicate about his nature, but it was better to accept it than to try to deny it.

He squeezed the bracelet gently and dropped his hand.

"Thank you, Sos," she murmured, and leaned over to kiss him on the neck.

16

WHEN HE WOKE AGAIN, HE SUS-PECTED THAT IT HAD BEEN A fantasy, like the oddities visible on the silent television, except that his bracelet was gone and his left wrist was pale where it had rested. This time he was alone, in another squared-off cabin, and feeling fit. Somehow he had been taken from the mountain and revived and left here, while his little friend Stupid had died. He could not guess the reason.

He got up and dressed, finding his clothing clean and whole, beside the bunk. If this were death, he thought, it was not unlike life. But that was foolishness; this was *not* death.

No food had been stocked, and there were no weapons upon the rack. As a matter of fact, the rack itself was absent. Sos opened the door, hoping to see familiar forest or landscape or even the base of the mountain—and found only a blank wall similar to the one he had traveled down in the vision. No vision after all, but reality.

"I'll be right with you, Sos." It was the voice of the little girl—the tiny woman who had teased him and outmaneuvered him and finally struck him down. His throat still ached, now that he thought of it, though not obtrusively. He looked at his bare wrist again.

Well, she had claimed to know what the bracelet meant.

She trotted down the hall, as small as ever, wearing a more shapely smock and smiling. Her hair, now visible, was brown and curly, and it contributed considerably to her femininity. The bracelet on her arm glittered; evidently she had polished it to make the gold return to life. He saw that it reached all the way around her wrist and overlapped slightly, while the mark it had left on his own wrist left a good quarter of the circle open. Had this tiny creature actually prevailed over him?

"Feeling better, Sos?" she inquired solicitously. "I know we gave you a rough time yesterday, but the doc says a period of exercise is best to saturate the system. So I saw that you got it."

He looked uncomprehendingly at her.

"Oh, that's right—you don't understand about our world yet." She smiled engagingly and took his arm. "You see, you were almost frozen in the snow, and we had to bring you around before permanent damage was done. Sometimes a full recovery takes weeks, but you were so healthy we gave you the energizer immediately. It's some kind of drug—I don't know much about these things— it scours out the system somehow and removes the damaged tissue. But it has to reach everywhere, the fingers and toes and things—well, I don't really understand it. But some good, strenuous calisthenics circulate it nicely. Then you sleep and the next thing you know you're better."

"I don't remember—"

"I put you to sleep, Sos. After I kissed you. It's just a matter of touching the right pressure points. I can show you, if—"

He declined hastily. She must have gotten him to the cabin room, too—or more likely had a man haul him there. Had she also undressed him and cleaned his clothing, as Sola had done so long ago? The similarities were disturbing.

"It's all right, Sos. I have your bracelet, remember? I didn't stay with you last night because I knew you'd be out for the duration, but I'll be with you from now on." She hesitated. "Unless you changed your mind?"

She was so little, more like a doll than a woman. Her concern was quite touching, but it was hard to know what to say. She was hardly half his weight. What could she know of the way of men and women?

"Oh, is that so!" she exclaimed, flashing, though he had not spoken. "Well, let's go back to your room right now and I'll show you I don't just climb ladders!"

He smiled at her vehemence. "No, keep it. I guess you know what you're doing." And he guessed he liked being chased, too.

She had guided him through right-angled corridors illuminated by overhead tubes of incandescence and on to another large room. There seemed to be no end to this odd enclosed world. He had yet to see honest daylight since coming here. "This is our cafeteria. We're just in time for mess."

There was a long counter with plates of food set upon it—thin slices of bacon, steaming oatmeal, poached eggs, sausage, toasted bread and other items he did not recognize. Farther down he saw cups of fruit juice, milk and hot drinks, as well as assorted jellies and spreads. It was as though someone had emptied the entire larder of a hostel and spread it out for a single feast. There was more than anyone could eat.

"Silly. You just take anything you want and put it on your tray," she said. "Here." She lifted a plastic tray from a stack at the end and handed it to him. She took one herself and preceded him down the aisle, selecting plates as she moved. He followed, taking one of each.

He ran out of tray space long before the end of the counter. "Here," she said, unconcerned. "Put some on mine."

The terminus opened into an extended dining area, square tables draped with overlapping white cloths. People were seated at several, finishing their meals. Both men and women wore coveralls and smocks similar to what he had seen already, making him feel out of place though he was normally dressed. Sosa led him to a vacant table and set the array of food and beverage upon it.

"I could introduce you to everyone, but we like to keep meals more or less private. If you want company, you leave the other chairs open; if you want to be left alone, tilt them up, like this." She leaned the two unused chairs forward against the sides of the table. "No one will bother us."

She viewed his array. "One thing, Sos—we don't waste anything. You eat everything you take."

He nodded. He was ravenous.

"We call this the underworld," she said as he ate, "but we don't consider ourselves criminals." She paused, but he didn't understand the allusion. "Anyway, we're all dead here. I mean, we all would have been dead if we hadn't—well, the same way you came. Climbing the mountain. I came last year. Just about every week there's someone—someone who makes it. Who doesn't turn back. So our population stays pretty steady."

Sos looked up over a mouthful. "Some turn back?"

"*Most* do. They get tired, or they change their minds, or something, and they go down again."

"But no one ever returns from the mountain!"

"That's right," she said uncomfortably.

He didn't press the matter, though he filed it away for future investigation.

"So we're really dead, because none of us will ever be seen in the world again. But we aren't idle. We work very hard, all of us. As soon as we're finished eating, I'll show you."

She did. She took him on a tour of the kitchen, where sweaty cooks worked full time preparing the plates of food and helpers ran the soiled dishes and trays through a puffing cleaning machine. She showed him the offices where accounts were kept. He did not grasp the purpose of such figuring, except that it was essential in some way to keep mining, manufacturing and exporting in balance. This made sense; he remembered the computations he had had to perform when training Sol's warriors, and this underworld was a far more complex community.

She took him to the observation deck, where men watched television screens and listened to odd sounds. The pictures were not those of the ordinary sets in the cabins, however, and this attracted his immediate interest.

"This is Sos," she said to the man in charge. "He arrived forty-eight hours ago. I—took him in charge."

"Sure—Sosa," the man replied, glancing at the bracelet. He shook Sos's hand. "I'm Tom. Glad to know you. Matter of fact, I recognize you. I brought you in. You certainly gave it a try!"

"Brought me in?" There was something strange and not altogether likeable about this man with the unusual name, despite his easy courtesy.

"I'll show you." Tom walked over to one of the screens that was blank. "This is a closed-circuit teevee covering the east slope of Helicon, down below the snowline." He turned it on, and Sos recognized the jumbled terrain he had navigated with the help of his rope. He had never seen a real picture on the television before—that is, one that applied to the present world, he corrected himself, and it fascinated him.

"Helicon—the mountain?" he asked, straining to remember where he had read of something by that name. "The home of . . . the muses?"

Tom faced him, and again there was a strangeness in his pale eyes. "Now how would you know that? Yes—since we remember the things of the old world here, we named it after—" He caught a signal from one of the others and turned quickly to the set. "There's one coming down now. Here, I'll switch to him."

That reminded Sos. "The ones that come down—where do they go?" He saw that Sosa had withdrawn from their conversation and was now showing off her bracelet to the other workers.

"I'm afraid you're about to find out, though you may not like it much," Tom said, watching him with a peculiar eagerness. Sos was careful not to react; these people obviously did not contest in the circle, but had their methods of trial. He was about to be subjected to something unpleasant.

Tom found his picture and brought the individual into focus. It was a middle-aged staffer, somewhat flabby. "He probably lost his woman to a younger warrior and decided to make the big play," Tom remarked without sympathy. "A lot are like that. There's something

about a broken romance that sends a man to the mountain." Sos's stomach tightened, but the man wasn't looking at him. "This one ascended to the snowline, then turned about when his feet got cold. Unless he changes his mind again pretty soon—"

"They do that?"

"Oh yes. Some waver half a dozen times. The thing is, the mountain is real. Death looks honorable from a distance, but the height and snow make it a matter of determination. Unless a man is really serious about dying, that climb will make him reconsider. He wonders whether things back home are quite so bad as he thought, whether he couldn't return and try again. If he's weak, he vacillates, and of course we don't want the quitters. It's natural selection, really, not that that would mean anything to you."

Sos refused to be drawn out by the condescending tone and assumptions of ignorance. It occurred to him that his general knowledge could be a hidden asset, in case things got ugly here.

"A man who carries his conviction all the way to the end is a man worth saving," Tom continued as the picture, evidently controlled by the motions of his fingers on the knobs, followed the staffer unerringly. "We want to be sure that he really has renounced life, and won't try to run back at the first opportunity. The ordeal of the mountain makes it clear. You were a good example—you charged right on up and never hesitated at all. You and that bird—too bad we couldn't save it, but it wouldn't have been happy here anyway. We saw you try to scare it away, and then it froze. I thought for a moment you were going to turn back then, but you didn't. Just as well, I liked your looks."

So all the agonies of his private demise had been observed by this cynical voyeur? Sos maintained the slightly stupid expression he had adopted since becoming suspicious, and watched the staffer pick his way along the upper margin of the projecting metal beams. There would be some later occasion, perhaps, to repay this mockery. "How did you—fetch me?"

"Put on a snowsuit and dragged you into the nearest hatch. Took three of us to haul the harness. You're a bull of a man, you know. After that—well, I guess you're already familiar with the revival procedure. We had to wait until you were all the way under; sometimes people make a last-minute effort to start down again. We don't bring them in if they're facing the wrong way, even if they freeze to death. It's the intent that counts. You know, you almost made it to the top. That's quite something, for an inexperienced climber."

"How did you know I wouldn't kill myself when I woke up?"

"Well, we can never be sure. But generally speaking, a person doesn't choose the mountain if he's the suicidal type. That sounds funny, I know, but it's the case. Anyone can kill himself, but only the mountain offers complete and official oblivion. When you ascend Helicon, you never come back. There is no news and no body. It's as though you have entered another world—perhaps a better one. You're not giving up, you're making an honorable departure. At least, that's the way I see it. The coward kills himself; the brave or devout man takes the mountain."

Much of this made sense to Sos, but he didn't care to admit it yet. "But you said some turn back."

"*Most* turn back. They're the ones who are doing it for bravado, or as a play for pity, or just plain foolishness. We don't need that kind here."

"What about that staffer out there now? If you don't take him in, where will he go?"

Tom frowned. "Yes, I'm afraid he really means to give up." He raised his voice. "Bill, you agree?"

"'Fraid so," the man addressed called back. "Better finish it; there's another at the base. No sense having him see it."

"This is not a pleasant business," Tom said, licking his lips with an anticipation that seemed to be, if not pleasure, a reasonable facsimile. "But you can't maintain a legend on nothing. So—" He activated another panel, and wavy crosshairs appeared on the screen. As he adjusted the dials the cross moved to center on the body of the staffer. He pulled a red handle.

A column of fire shot out from somewhere offscreen and engulfed the man. Sos jumped, but realized that he could do nothing. For a full minute the terrible blaze seared on the screen; then Tom lifted the handle and it stopped.

A blackened mound of material was all that remained.

"Flamethrower," Tom explained pleasantly.

Sos had seen death before, but this appalled him. The killing had been contrary to all his notions of honor; no warning, no circle, no sorrow. "You mean—if I had—?"

Tom faced him, the light from the screen reflecting from the whites of his eyes in miniature skull-shapes. This was the question he had been waiting for. "Yes."

Sosa was tugging at his arm. "That's enough," she said. "Come on, Sos. We had to show you. It isn't all bad."

"What if I decide to leave this place?" he demanded, sickened by such calculated murder.

She pulled him on. "Don't talk like that. Please."

So that was the way it stood, he thought. They had not been joking when they named this the land of the dead. Some were dead figuratively, and some dead inside. But what had he expected when he ventured upon the mountain? Life and pleasure?

"Where are the women?" he inquired as they traveled the long passages.

"There aren't many. The mountain is not a woman's way. The few we have are—shared."

"Then why did you take my bracelet?"

She increased her pace. "I'll tell you, Sos, really I will—but not right now, all right?"

They entered a monstrous workshop. Sos had been impressed by the crazies' "shop," but this dwarfed it as the underworld complex dwarfed an isolated hostel. Men were laboring with machines in long lines, stamping and shaping metal objects. "Why," he exclaimed, "those are weapons!"

"Well, *someone* has to make them, I suppose. Where did you think they came from?

"The crazies always—"

"The truth is we mine some metals and salvage some, and turn out the implements. The crazies distribute them and send us much of our food in return. I thought you understood about that when I showed you the accounting section. We also exchange information. They're what you call the service part of the economy, and we're the manufacturing part. The nomads are the consumers. It's all very nicely balanced, you see."

"But *why*?" It was the same question he had asked at the school.

"That's something each person has to work out for himself."

And the same answer. "You sound like Jones."

"Jones?"

"My crazy instructor. He taught me how to read."

She halted, surprised. "Sos! You can *read*?"

"I was always curious about things." He hadn't meant to reveal his literacy. Still, he could hardly have concealed it indefinitely.

"Would you show me how? We have so many books here—"

"It isn't that simple. It takes years to learn."

"We have years, Sos. Come, I want to start right away." She fairly dragged him in a new direction, despite the disparity in their sizes. She had delightful energy.

It was easy to recognize the library. In many respects the underworld resembled the crazies' building. "Jim, this is Sos. He can read!"

The spectacled man jumped up, smiling. "Marvelous!" He looked Sos up and down, then, a trifle dubiously. "You look more like a warrior than a scholar. No offense."

"Can't a warrior read?"

Jim fetched a book. "A formality, Sos— but would you read from this? Just a sample passage, please."

Sos took the volume and opened it at random. "BRUTUS: Our course will seem too bloody, Caius Cassius, To cut the head off and then to hack the limbs, Like wrath in death and envy afterwards; for Anthony is but a limb of Caesar; Let us be sacrificers, but not butchers, Caius. We all stand up against the spirit of Caesar; And in the spirit of men there is no blood; O! that we then—"

"Enough! Enough!" Jim cried. "You can read, you can read, you certainly can. Have you been assigned yet? We must have you in the library! There is so much to—"

"You can give classes in reading," Sosa added excitedly. "We all want to learn, but so few know how—"

"I'll call Bob immediately. What a discovery!" The librarian fumbled for the intercom on his desk.

"Let's get out of here," Sos said, embarrassed by the commotion. He had always considered reading a private pursuit, except in the school, and found this eagerness upsetting.

It was a long day in the perpetual artificiality of the underworld, and he was glad to retire at the end of it. He was hardly certain he wanted to spend the rest of his life under the mountain, extraordinary as this world might be.

"But it really isn't a bad life, Sos," she said. "You get used to it—and the things we do are really important. We're the manufacturers for the continent; we make all the weapons, all the basic furnishings for the hostels, the prefabricated walls and floors, the appliances and electronic equipment—"

"Why did you take my bracelet?"

The question brought her up short. "Well, as I said, there aren't many women here. They have it scheduled so that each man has a night with someone each week. It isn't quite like a full-time relationship, but on the other hand there is variety. It works out pretty well."

The game of traveling bracelets. Yes, he could imagine how certain people would enjoy that, though he had noticed that most men did not use the golden signals here. "Why am I excluded?"

"Well you *can*, if you want. I thought—"

"I'm not objecting, girl. I just want to know why. Why do I rate a full-time partner when there aren't enough to go around?"

Her lip trembled. "Do—do you want it back?" She touched the bracelet.

He grabbed her, unresisting, and pressed her down upon the bunk. She met his kiss eagerly. "No I *don't* want it back. I—oh, get that smock off, then!" What use to demand reason of a woman?

She divested herself of her clothing, all of it, with alacrity. Then, womanlike, she seemed to change her mind. "Sos—"

He had expected something like this. "Go ahead."

"I'm barren."

He watched her silently.

"I tried—many bracelets. Finally I had the crazies check me. I can never have a baby of my own, Sos. That's why I came to the mountain . . . but babies are even more important here. So—"

"So you went after the first man they hauled off the mountain."

"Oh, no, Sos. I took my turn on the list. But when there isn't any love *or* any chance for—well, some complained I was unresponsive, and there really didn't seem to be much point in it. So

Bob put me on the revival crew, where I could meet new people. The one who is on duty when someone is brought in is, well, responsible. To explain everything and make him feel at home and get him suitably situated. You know. You're the nineteenth person I've handled—seventeen men and two women. Some of them were old, or bitter. You're the first I really—that sounds even worse, doesn't it!"

Young, strong, pliable: the answer to a lonely woman's dreams, he thought. Yet why not? He had no inclination to embrace assorted women in weekly servicings. Better to stick to one, one who might understand if his heart were elsewhere.

"Suppose I happen to want a child of my own?"

"Then you—take back your bracelet."

He studied her, sitting beside him, halfway hiding behind the balled smock as though afraid to expose herself while the relationship was in doubt. She was very small and very woman-shaped. He thought about what it meant to be denied a child, and began to understand as he had not understood before what had driven Sol.

"I came to the mountain because I could not have the woman I loved," he said. "I know all that is gone, now—but my heart doesn't. I can offer you only—friendship."

"Then give me that," she said, dropping the smock.

He took her into the bed with him, holding her as carefully as he had held Stupid, afraid of crushing her. He held her passively at first, thinking that that would be the extent of it. He was wrong. But it was Sola his mind embraced.

17

BOB WAS A TALL, AGGRESSIVE MAN, THE MANIFEST LEADER of the mountain group. "I understand you can read," he said at once. "How come?"

Sos explained about his schooling.

"Too bad."

Sos waited for him to make his point.

"Too bad it wasn't the next one. We could have used your talent here."

Sos still waited. This was like taking the circle against an unknown weapon. Bob did not have the peculiar aura of the death-dealing Tom, but he was named as strangely and struck Sos as thoroughly ruthless. He wondered how common this stamp was among those who had renounced life. It probably was typical; he had seen for himself how the manner, the personality of the leader, transmitted itself to the group. Sos had shaped Sol's empire with tight organization and a touch of humor, letting the men enjoy their competition for points as they improved their skills. When he left, Tyl had ruled, and the discipline remained without the humor. The camps had become grim places. Strange that he only saw this now!

"We have a special and rather remarkable assignment for you," Bob was saying. "A unique endeavor."

Seeing that Sos was not going to commit himself, Bob got down to specifics. "We are not entirely ignorant of affairs on the surface, can't afford to be. Our information is largely second hand, of course—our teevee perceptors don't extend far beyond the Helicon environs—but we have a much better overall view than you primitives have. There's an empire building up there. We have to break it up in a hurry."

Evidently that excellent overall view did not reveal Sos's own place in the scheme. He suspected more strongly now that it would be best if it never were known. The flamethrower undoubtedly pointed in the direction of the organizer of such an empire, while an ignorant, if literate, primitive was safe. "How do you know?"

"You have not heard of it?" The contempt was veiled and perhaps unconscious; it had not occurred to Bob that a newcomer could know more than he. The question had lulled any suspicions he might have had and strengthened his preconceptions. "It's run by one Sol, and it's been expanding enormously this past year. Several of our recent arrivals have had news of it, and there's even been word from the South American unit. Very wide notoriety."

"South America?" Sos had read about this, the continent of pre-Blast years, along with Africa and Asia, but had no evidence it still existed.

"Did you think we were the only such outfit in the world? There's one or more Helicons on every continent. We have lines connecting us to all of them, and once in a while we exchange personnel, though there is a language barrier. South America is more advanced than we are; they weren't hit so hard in the war. We have a Spanish-speaking operator, and quite a few of theirs speak English, so there's no trouble there. But that's a long ways away; when *they* get wind of an empire here, it's time to do something about it."

"Why?"

"Why do you think? What would happen to the status quo if the primitives started really organizing? Producing their own food and weapons, say? There'd be no control over them at all!"

Sos decided that further questions along this line would be dangerous. "Why me?"

"Because you're the biggest, toughest savage to descend upon us in a long time. You bounced back from your exposure on the mountain in record time. If anyone can take it, you can. We need a strong body now, and you're it."

It occurred to Sos that it had been a long time since this man had practiced diplomacy, if ever. "It for *what*?"

"It to return to life. To take over that empire."

If Bob had intended to shock him, he had succeeded. To return to life! To go back . . . "I'm not your man. I have sworn never to bear a weapon again." That was not precisely true, but if they expected him to face Sol again, it certainly applied. He had agreed never to bring a weapon against Sol again—and regardless of other circumstances, he meant to abide by the terms of their last encounter. It was a matter of honor, in life or death.

"You take such an oath seriously?" But Bob's sneer faded as he looked at Sos. "Well, what if we train you to fight without weapons?"

"Without a weapon—in the *circle*?"

"With the bare hands. The way your little girl does. That doesn't violate any of your precious vows, does it? Why are you so reluctant? Don't you realize what this means to you? You will have an empire!"

Sos was infuriated by the tone and implications, but realized that he could not protest further without betraying himself. This was big; the moment Bob caught on—

"What if I refuse? I came to the mountain to die."

"I think you know that there is no refusal here. But if personal pressure or pain doesn't faze you, as I hope it doesn't, there may be things that will. This won't mean much to you right now, but if you think about it for a while you'll come around, I suspect." And Bob told him some things that vindicated Sos's original impression of him utterly.

Not for the reason the underground master thought—but Sos was committed.

"To *life*?" Sosa demanded incredulously, when he told her later. "But no one ever goes back!"

"I will be the first—but I will do it anonymously."

"But if you want to return, why did you come to the mountain? I mean—"

"I don't want to return. I have to."

"But—" She was at a loss for words for a moment. "Did Bob threaten you? You shouldn't let him—"

"It was not a chance I could afford to take."

She looked at him, concerned. "Was it to—to harm *her*? The one you—"

"Something like that."

"And if you go, you'll get her back."

After his experience in the observation deck, Sos was aware that anything he said or did might be observed in this region. He could not tell Sosa anything more than Bob thought he knew. "There is an empire forming out there. I have to go and eliminate its leader. But it won't

be for a year or more, Sosa. It will take me that long to get ready. I have a lot to learn first."

Bob thought he had been swayed, among other things, by the dream of owning an empire. Bob must never know where his real loyalty lay. If someone were sent to meet Sol, it was best that it be a friend. . . .

"May I keep your bracelet—that year?"

"Keep it forever, Sosa. You will be training me."

She contemplated him sadly. "Then it wasn't really an accident, our meeting. Bob knew what you would be doing before we brought you in. He set it up."

"Yes." Again, it was close enough.

"Damn him!" she cried. "That was cruel!"

"It was necessary, according to his reasoning. He took the most practical way to do what had to be done. You and I merely happen to be the handiest tools. I'm sorry."

"*You're* sorry!" she muttered. Then she smiled, making the best of it. "At least we know where we stand."

She trained him. She taught him the blows and the holds she knew, laboriously learned in childhood from a tribe that taught its women self-defense— and cast out the barren ones. Men, of course, disdained the weaponless techniques—but they also disdained to accept any woman who was an easy mark, and so the secret knowledge passed from mother to daughter: how to destroy a man.

Sos did not know what inducement Bob had used to make Sosa reveal these tactics to a man, and did not care to inquire.

She showed him how to strike with his hands with such power as to sunder wooden beams, and how to smash them with his bare feet, and his elbow, and his head. She made him understand the vulnerable points of the human body, the places where a single blow could stun or maim or kill. She had him run at her as though in a rage, and she brought him down again and again, feet and arms tangled uselessly. She let him try to choke her, and she broke that hold in half a dozen painful and embarrassing ways, though there was more strength in his two thumbs than in her two hands. She showed him the pressure points that were open to pain, the nerve centers where pressure induced paralysis or unconsciousness. She demonstrated submission holds that she could place on him with a single slender arm, that held him in such agony he could neither break nor fight. She brought out the natural weapons of the body, so basic they were almost forgotten by men: the teeth, the nails, the extended fingers, the bone of the skull, even the voice.

And when he had mastered these things and learned to avoid and block the blows and break or nullify the holds and counter the devious strategies of weaponless combat, she showed him how to fight when portions of his body were incapacitated: one arm, two arms, the legs, the eyes. He stalked her blindfolded, with feet tied together, with weights tied to his limbs, with medicine to make him dizzy. He climbed the hanging ladder with arms bound in a straitjacket; he swung through the elevated bars with one arm shackled to one foot. He stood still while she delivered the blows that had brought him down during their first encounter, only twisting almost imperceptibly to take them harmlessly.

Then he set it all aside. He went to the operating room and exposed himself to the anesthetics and the scalpels. The surgeon placed flexible plastic panels under the skin of his belly and lower back, tough enough to halt the driven blade of knife or sword. He placed a collar upon Sos's neck that locked with a key, and braced the long bones of arms and legs with metallic rods, and embedded steel mesh in the crotch. He mutilated the face, rebuilding the nose with stronger stuff and filling the cheeks with nylon weave. He ground and capped the teeth. He peeled back the forehead and resodded with shaped metal.

Sundry other things occurred in successive operations before they turned him loose to start again. No part of him was recognizable as the man once known as Sos; instead he walked slowly, as a juggernaut rolls, fighting against the pain of an ugly rebirth.

He resumed training. He worked on the devices in the rec room, now more familiar to him than his new body. He climbed the ladder, swung on the bars, lifted the weights. He walked up and down the hallways, balancing his suddenly heavier torso and increasing his pace gradually until he was able to run without agony. He hardened his healing hands and feet by smashing the boards; in time he developed monstrously thick calluses. He stood still, this time not moving at all, while Sosa struck his stomach, neck and head with all her strength—with a staff—and he laughed.

Then with a steeltrap motion he caught the weapon from her inexpert grasp and bent it into an S shape by a single exertion of his two trunklike wrists. He pinioned her own wrists, both together, with the fingers and thumb of one hand and lifted her gently off the floor, smiling.

Sosa jackknifed and drove both heels against his exposed chin. "Ouch!" she screamed. "That's like landing on a chunk of stone!"

He chuckled and draped her unceremoniously across his right shoulder while hefting his weight and hers upon the bottom rung of the ladder with that same right arm. She writhed and jammed stiffened fingers into his left shoulder just inside the collarbone. "You damned gorilla," she complained. "You've got calluses over your pressure points!"

"Nylon calluses," he said matter-of-factly. "I could break a gorilla in two." His voice was harsh; the collar constricting his throat destroyed any dulcet utterances he attempted.

"You're still a great ugly beast!" she said, clamping her teeth hard upon the lobe of his ear and chewing.

"Ugly as hell," he agreed, turning his head so that she was compelled to release her bite or have her neck stretched painfully.

"Awful taste," she whispered as she let go. "I love you."

He reversed rotation, and she jammed her lips against his face and kissed him furiously. "Take me back to our room, Sos," she said. "I want to feel needed."

He obliged, but the aftermath was not entirely harmonious. "You're still thinking of *her*," she accused him. "Even when we're—"

"That's all over," he said, but the words lacked conviction.

"It's *not* over! It hasn't even begun yet. You still love her and you're going back!"

"It's an assignment. You know that."

"*She* isn't the assignment. It's almost time for you to go, and I'll never see you again, and you can't even tell me you love me."

"I do love you."

"But not as much as you love her."

"Sosa, she is hardly fit to be compared to you. You're a warm, wonderful girl, and I would love you much more, in time. I'm going back, but I want you to keep my bracelet. How else can I convince you?"

She wrapped herself blissfully about him. "I know it, Sos. I'm a demented jealous bitch. It's just that I'm losing you forever, and I can't stand it. The rest of my life without you—"

"Maybe I'll send a replacement." But it ceased to be funny as he said it.

After a moment she brightened slightly. "Let's do it again, Sos. Every minute counts."

"Hold on, woman! I'm not *that* sort of a superman!"

"Yes you are," she said. And she proved him wrong again.

18

NAMELESS AND WEAPONLESS, HE MARCHED. IT WAS SPRING, almost two years after he had journeyed dejectedly toward the mountain. Sos had gone to oblivion; the body that clothed his brain today was a different one, his face a creation of the laboratory, his voice a croak. Plastic contacts made his eyes stare out invulnerably, and his hair sprouted without pigment.

Sos was gone—but secret memories remained within the nameless one, surging irrepressibly when evoked by familiar sights. He was anonymous but not feelingless. It was almost possible to forget, as he traveled alone, missing the little bird on his shoulder, that he came as a machine of destruction. He could savor the forest trails and friendly cabins just as the young sworder had four years ago. A life and death ago!

He stood beside the circle: the one where Sol the sword had fought Sol of all weapons for name and armament and, as it turned out, woman. What a different world it would have been, had that encounter never taken place!

He entered the cabin, recognizing the underworld manufacture and the crazy maintenance. Strange how his perceptions had changed! He had never really wondered before where the supplies had come from; he, like most nomads, had taken such things for granted. How had such naïveté, been possible?

He broke out supplies and prepared a Gargantuan meal for himself. He had to eat enormously to maintain this massive body, but food was not much of a pleasure. Taste had been one of the many things that had suffered in the cause of increased power. He wondered whether, in the past, the surgeons had been able to perform their miracles without attendant demolition of peripheral sensitivity. Or had their machines taken the place of warriors?

A girl showed up at dusk, young enough and pretty enough, but when she saw his bare wrist she kept to herself. Hostels had always been excellent places to hunt for bracelets. He wondered whether the crazies knew about this particular aspect of their service.

He slept in one bunk, the girl courteously taking the one adjacent though she could have claimed privacy by establishing herself on the far side of the column. She glanced askance when she perceived that he was after all alone, but she was not concerned. His readings had also told him that before the Blast women had had to watch out for men, and seldom dared to sleep in the presence of a stranger. If that were true—though it was hardly creditable in a civilization more advanced than the present one—things had certainly improved. It was unthinkable that a man require favors not freely proffered—or that a woman should withhold them capriciously. Yet Sosa had described the perils of her childhood, where tribes viewed women differently; not all the badness had been expunged by the fire.

The girl could contain her curiosity no longer. "Sir, if I may ask—where is your woman?"

He thought of Sosa, pert little Sosa, almost too small to carry a full-sized bracelet, but big in performance and spirit. He missed her. "She is in the world of the dead," he said.

"I'm sorry," she said, misunderstanding as he had meant her to. A man buried his bracelet with his wife, if he loved her, and did not take another until mourning was over. How was he to explain that it was not Sosa's death, but his own return to life that had parted them forever?

The girl sat up in her bed, touching her nightied breast and showing her embarrassment. Her hair was pale. "It was wrong of me to ask," she said.

"It was wrong of me not to explain," he said graciously, knowing how ugly he would appear to this innocent.

"If you desire to—"

"No offense," he said with finality.

"None," she agreed, relieved.

Would this ordinary, attractive, artless girl sharing his cabin but not his bed— would she ever generate the violence of passion and sorrow he had known? Would some stout naïve warrior hand her his bracelet tomorrow and travel to the mountain when he lost her?

It was possible, for that was the great modern dream of life and love. There was in the least of people, male and female, the capacity to arouse tumultuous emotion. That was the marvel and the glory of it all.

She fixed his breakfast in the morning, another courteous gesture that showed she had been well brought up. She tried not to stare as he stepped out of the shower. He blessed her and went his way, and she hers. These customs were good, and had they met four years ago and she been of age then—

It took him only a week to cover the distance two men and a girl traveled before. Some of the cabins were occupied, others not, but he kept to himself and was left alone. It surprised him a little that common manners had changed; this was another quality of the nomad society that he had never properly appreciated until he learned how blunt things could be elsewhere.

But there were some changes. The markers were gone; evidently the crazies, perhaps prompted by his report to Jones, had brought their Geiger clickers (manufactured in the underworld electronics shop) and resurveyed the area at last. That could mean that the moths and shrews were gone, too, or at least brought into better harmony with the rest of the ecology. He saw the tracks of hoofed animals and was certain of it.

The old camp remained, replete with its memories—and it was still occupied! Men exercised in the several circles and the big tent had been maintained beside the river. The firetrench, however, had been filled in, the retrenchments leveled; this was the decisive evidence that the shrews no longer swarmed. They had finally given way to the stronger species: man.

But back nearer the fringe of the live radiation, where man could not go—who ruled there? And if there should ever be another Blast. . . .

Why was he surprised to find men here? He had known this would be the case; that was why he had come first to this spot. This had been the birthing place of the empire.

He approached the camp and was promptly challenged. "Halt! Which tribe are you bound to?" a hefty staffer demanded, eyeing his tunic as though trying to identify his weapon.

"No tribe. Let me see your leader."

"What's your name?"

"I am nameless. Let me see your leader."

The staffer scowled. "Stranger, you're overdue for a lesson in manners."

Sos reached out slowly and put one hand under the staff. He lifted.

"Hey, what are you—!" But the man had either to let go or to follow; he could not overcome. In a moment he was reaching for the sky, as Sos's single arm forced the staff and both the man's hands up.

Sos twisted with contemptuous gravity, and the staffer was wrenched around helplessly. "If you do not take me to your master, I will carry you there myself." He brought the weapon down suddenly and the man fell, still clinging to it.

Others had collected by this time to stare. Sos brought up his other hand, shifted his grip to the two ends of the rod, while the staffer foolishly hung on, bent it into a splendid half-circle. He let go, leaving the useless instrument in the hands of its owner.

Very shortly, he was ushered into the leader's presence.

It was Sav.

"What can I do for you, strongster?" Sav inquired, not recognizing him under the mauled features and albino hair. "Things are pretty busy right now, but if you come to enlist—"

"What you can do for me is to identify yourself and your tribe and turn both over to me." For once he was glad of the harshness inherent in his voice.

Sav laughed good-naturedly. "I'm Sav the Staff, in charge of staff-training for Sol, master of empire. Unless you come from Sol, I'm turning nothing over to you."

"I do not come from Sol. I come to vanquish him and rule in his stead."

"Just like that, huh? Well, mister nameless, you can start here. We'll put up a man against you in the circle, and you'll either take him or join our tribe. What's your weapon?"

"I have no weapon but my hands."

Sav studied him with interest. "Now, let me get this straight. You don't have a name, you don't have a tribe and you don't have a weapon—but you figure to take over this camp?"

"Yes."

"Well, maybe I'm a little slow today, but I don't quite follow how you plan to do that."

"I will break you in the circle."

Sav burst out laughing. "Without a weapon?"

"Are you afraid to meet me?"

"Mister, I wouldn't meet you if you *had* a weapon. Not unless you had a tribe the size of this one to put up against it. Don't you know the rules?"

"I had hoped to save time."

Sav looked at him more carefully. "You know, you remind me of someone. Not your face, not your voice . . . You—"

"Select some man to meet me, then, and I will take him and all that follow him from you, until the tribe is mine."

Sav's look was pitying now. "You really want to tackle a trained staffer in the circle? With your bare hands?"

Sos nodded.

"This goes against the grain, but all right then." He summoned one of his men and showed the way to a central circle.

The selected staffer was embarrassed. "But he has no weapon!" he exclaimed.

"Just knock him down a couple of times," Sav advised. "He insists on doing it." Men were gathering; word had spread of Sos's feat with the guard's staff.

Sos removed his tunic and stood in short trunks and bare feet.

The bystanders gasped. The tunic had covered him from chin to knee and elbow, exposing little more than the hands and feet. The others had assumed that he was a large, chubby man, old because of the color of his hair and the leathery texture of his face. They had been curious about the strength he had shown, but not really convinced it had not been a fluke effort.

"Biceps like clubheads!" someone exclaimed. "Look at that neck!" Sos no longer wore the metal collar; now his neck was a solid mass of horny callus and scar tissue. The staffer assigned to meet him stood openmouthed.

Sav pulled the man back. "Gom, take the circle," he said tersely.

A much larger staffer came forward, his body scarred and discolored by many encounters: a veteran. He held his weapon ready and stepped into the circle without hesitation.

Sos entered and stood with hands on hips.

Gom had no foolish scruples. He feinted several times to see what the nameless one would do, then landed a vicious blow to the side of the neck.

Sos stood unmoved.

The staffer looked at his weapon, shrugged, and struck again.

After standing for a full minute, Sos moved. He advanced on Gom, reached out almost casually for the staff, and spun it away with a sharp twist of one wrist. He hurled it out of the circle.

Sos had never touched the man physically, but the staffer was out of business. He had tried to hold on to his weapon. Gom's fingers were broken.

"I have one man, and myself," Sos announced. "My man is not ready to fight again, so I will fight next for two."

Shaken, Sav sent in another warrior, designating a third as collateral. Sos caught the two ends of the staff and held them while the man tried vainly to free it. Finally Sos twisted and the weapon buckled. He let go and stepped back.

The man stood holding the S-shaped instrument, dazed. Sos only had to touch him with a finger, and the staffer stumbled out of the circle.

"I have four men, counting myself. I will match for four."

By this time the entire camp was packed around the circle. "You have already made your point," Sav said. "I will meet you."

"Yourself and your entire tribe against what I have here?" Sos inquired, mocking him.

"My skill against your skill," Sav said, refusing to be ruffled. "My group— against your service and complete information about yourself. Who you are, where you came from, how you learned to fight like that, who sent you here."

"My service you may have, if you win it, or my life—but I am sworn to secrecy about the rest. Name other terms."

Sav picked up his staff. "Are you afraid to meet me?"

The men chuckled. Sav had nicely turned the dialogue on him. Who mocked whom?

"I cannot commit that information to the terms of the circle. I have no right."

"You have shown us your strength. We are curious. You ask me to put up my entire camp—but you won't even agree to put up your history. I don't think you really want to fight, stranger." The gathered men agreed vociferously, enjoying the exchange.

Sos appreciated certain qualities of leadership he had never recognized in Sav before. Sav had surely seen that he must lose if he entered the circle, and be shamed if he didn't. Yet he was forcing Sos to back off. Sav could refuse to do battle unless his terms were met, and do so with honor—and the word would quickly spread to Sol's other tribal leaders. It was a tactical masterstroke.

He would have to compromise. "All right," he said. "But I will tell only you. No one else."

"But *I* will tell whom I please!" Sav specified.

Sos did not challenge that. He had to hope that, if by some mischance he lost, he could still convince Sav in private of the necessity for secrecy. Sav was a sensible, easygoing individual; he would certainly listen and think before acting.

It was too bad that the smiling staffer had to be hurt by his friend.

Sav entered the circle. He had improved; his staff was blindingly swift and unerringly placed. Sos tried to catch the weapon and could not. The man had profited from observation of the two lesser warriors, and never let his staff stand still long enough to be grabbed. He also wasted no effort striking the column of gristle. He maneuvered instead for face shots, hoping to blind his antagonist, and rapped at elbows and wrists and feet. He also kept moving, as though certain that so solid a body would tire soon.

It was useless. Sos sparred a few minutes so that the staffer would not lose face before his men, then blocked the flying shaft and caught Sav's forearm. He yanked it to him and brought his other hand to bear.

There was a crack.

Sos let go and shoved the man out of the circle. No warrior present could mistake the finality of a dripping compound fracture. Men took hold of Sav as he staggered, hauled at his arm and set the exposed bone in place and bound the terrible wound in gauze, while Sos watched impassively from the circle.

It had not been strictly necessary. He could have won in a hundred kinder ways. But he had needed a victory that was serious and totally convincing. Had Sav lost indecisively, or by some trick blow that made him stumble from the circle like an intoxicated person, unmarked, the gathered witnesses would have been quick to doubt his capability or desire to fight, and the job would be unfinished. The break was tangible; Sav's men knew immediately that no one could have succeeded where their leader had failed, and that there had been no collusion and no cowardice.

Sos had inflicted dreadful pain, knowing that his erstwhile friend could bear it, in order to preserve what was more important: the loser's reputation.

"Put your second-in-command in charge of this camp," Sos snapped at Sav, showing no softness. "You and I take the trail—tomorrow morning, alone."

19

TWO MEN MOVED OUT, ONE WITH HIS ARM IN CAST AND SLING. They marched as far as the broken arm and loss of blood permitted, and settled into a hostel for the evening, without company.

"Why?" Sav inquired as Sos fixed supper.

"Why the arm?"

"No. I understand that. Why you?"

"I have been assigned to take over Sol's empire. He will hardly meet me in the circle until I bring down his chief lieutenants."

Sav leaned back carefully, favoring the arm. "I mean why *you*—Sos?"

First man, second day. He had betrayed himself already.

"You can trust me," Sav said. "I never told anyone about your nights with Sola, and I wasn't bound by the circle code then, not to you, I mean. I won't tell anyone now. The information belonged to me only if I won it from you, and I didn't."

"How did you know?"

"Well, I did room with you quite a spell, remember. I got to know you pretty well, and not just by sight. I know how you think and how you smell. I was awake some last night—little ache in my arm—and I walked by your tent."

"How did you know me sleeping when you did not know me awake?"

Sav smiled. "I recognized your snore."

"My—" He hadn't even known he snored.

"And one or two other things fit into place," Sav continued. "Like the way you stared at the spot on the ground where our little tent used to be—and I know you weren't remembering me! And the way you hummed 'Red River Valley' today while we marched, same way Sola used to hum 'Greensleeves,' even if you do carry a tune even worse than you did before. And the way you took care to make me look good in the circle, make me lose like a man. You didn't have to do that. You were taking care of me, same way I took care of you before."

"You took care of me?"

"You know—keeping the gals away from your tent all winter, even if I had to service 'em myself. Sending a man to bring Sol back when it was time. Stuff like that."

Sol had stayed away . . . until Sola was pregnant!

"You knew about Sol?"

"I'm just naturally nosy, I guess. But I can keep my mouth shut."

"You certainly can!" Sos took a moment to adjust himself to the changed situation. The staffer was a lot more knowledgeable and discreet than he had ever suspected. "All right, Sav. I'll tell you everything—and you can tell me how to keep my secrets so that nobody *else* catches on. Fair enough?"

"Deal! Except—"

"No exceptions. I can't tell anyone else."

"Except a couple are going to know anyway, no way to stop it. You get within a hundred feet of Sol, he'll know you. He's that way. And you won't fool Sola long, either. The others—well, if we can fake out Tor, no problem."

Sav was probably right. Somehow the thought did not disturb Sos; if he did his honest best to conceal his identity, but was known by those closest to him anyway, he could hardly be blamed. The word would not spread.

"You asked 'why me?' That's the same question I asked myself. They put pressure on me, but it wouldn't have been enough if I hadn't had internal doubts. Why me? The answer is, because I built the empire, though they didn't know that. I started it, I organized it, I trained it, I left men after me who could keep it rolling. If it is wrong, then I have a moral obligation to dismantle it—and I may be the only one who can do it without calamitous bloodshed. I am the only one who really understands its nature and the key individuals within it—and who can defeat Sol in the circle."

"Maybe you better start at the beginning," Sav said. "You went away, then I heard you came back with the rope, and Sol beat you and you went to the mountain—"

It was late at night by the time the complete story had been told.

Tyl's camp was much larger than Sav's had been. This was an acquisition tribe, contrasted to the training tribe, and by itself numbered almost five hundred warriors. This time there was no stupidity at the entrance; Sav was a ranking member of the hierarchy, and there was the unmistakable ring of command in his normally gentle voice as he cut through obstacles. Ten minutes after they entered the camp they stood before Tyl himself.

"What brings you here unattended, comrade?" Tyl inquired cautiously, not commenting on the mending arm. He looked older, but no less certain of himself.

"I serve a new master. This is the nameless one, who sought me out and defeated me in the circle. Now he offers me and my tribe against you and yours."

Tyl contemplated Sos's tunic, trying to penetrate to the body beneath it. "With all due respect, ex-comrade, my tribe is more powerful than yours. He will have to meet my subchiefs first."

"Of course. Post a third of your tribe to correspond to mine. After the nameless one defeats your man, he will match both sections against the remainder. You can study him today and meet him tomorrow."

"You seem to have confidence in him," Tyl observed.

Sav turned to Sos. "Master, if you would remove your dress—"

Sos obliged, finding it easy to let Sav handle things. The man certainly had talent for it. This early acquisition had been most fortunate.

Tyl looked. "I see," he said, impressed. "And what is his weapon?" Then, "I see," again.

That afternoon Sos knocked out the subchief sworder with a single hammerblow of one fist to the mid-section. He had the sword by the blade, having simply caught it in midthrust and held it. A slight crease showed along the callus covering the metallic mesh embedded in his palm where the edge had cut; that was all. He had closed upon the blade carefully, but the witnesses had not been aware of that. They had assumed that he had actually halted the full thrust with an unprotected hand.

Tyl, like Sav, was quick to learn. He, too, employed the sword, and he fenced with Sos's hands as though they were daggers, and with his head as though it were a club, and he kept his distance. It was wise strategy. The singing blade maintained an expert defense, and Tyl never took a chance.

But he forgot one thing: Sos had feet as well as hands and head. A sharp kick to the kneecap brought temporary paralysis there, interfering with mobility. Tyl knew he had lost, then, for even a narrow advantage inevitably grew, but he fought on, no coward. Not until both knees were dislocated did he attempt the suicide plunge.

Sos left the blade sticking in his upper arm and touched his fingers to the base of Tyl's exposed neck, and it was over.

Then he withdrew the blade and bound the wound together himself. It had been a stab, not a slash, and the metal reinforcement within the bone had stopped the point. The arm would heal.

When Tyl could walk, Sos added him to the party. They set out for the next major tribe, getting closer to Sol's own camp. Tyl traveled with his family, since Sos had not guaranteed any prompt return to the tribe, and Tyla took over household chores. The children stared at the man who had defeated their father, hardly able to accept it. They were too young yet to appreciate all the facts of battle, and had not understood that Tyl had been defeated at the time he joined Sol's nascent group. There were no frank conversations along the way. Tyl did not recognize the nameless one, and Sav cleverly nullified dangerous remarks.

They caught up to Tor's tribe after three weeks. Sos had determined that he needed one more leader in his retinue before he had enough to force Sol into the circle. He now had authority over more than six hundred men—but eight tribes remained, some very large. Sol could still preserve his empire by refusing to let these tribes accept the challenge and by refraining from circle combat himself. But acquisition of a third tribe should make Sos's chunk of empire too big to let go. . . .

Tor's tribe was smaller than Tyl's and more loosely organized, but still a formidable spread. A certain number of doubles teams were practicing, as though the encounter with the Pits had come out about even. Sos expected competent preparations for his coming, and was not disappointed. Tor met him promptly and took him into private conference, leaving Sav and Tyl out of it.

"I see you are a family man," he said.

Sos glanced at his bare wrist. "I was once a family man."

"Oh, I see." Tor, searching for weakness, had missed. "Well, I understand you came out of nowhere, defeated Sav and Tyl and mean to challenge Sol for his empire—and that you actually enter the circle without a weapon."

"Yes."

"It would seem foolish for me to meet you personally, since Tyl is a better fighter than I."

Sos did not comment.

"Yet it is not in my nature to avoid a challenge. Suppose we do this: I will put my tribe up against yours if you will meet my representative."

"One of your subchiefs? I will not put up six hundred men against a minor." But Sos's real concern was whether Tor recognized him.

"I did not say that. I said my representative, who is not a member of my group, against you, alone. If he beats you, you will release your men and go your way; Sol will reconquer them in time. If you overcome him, I will turn over my group to you, but I will remain in the service of Sol. I do not care to serve any other master at this time."

"This is a curious proposition." There had to be a hidden aspect to it, since Tor was always clever.

"Friend, *you* are a curious proposition."

Sos considered it, but discovered nothing inherently unfair about the terms. If he won, he had the tribe. If he lost, he was still free to try for Sol at a later date. It did not matter whom he fought; he would have to defeat the man sooner or later anyway, to prevent resurgence of the empire under some new master.

And it seemed that Tor did *not* recognize him, which was a private satisfaction. Perhaps he had worried too much about that.

"Very well. I will meet this man."

"He will be here in a couple of days. I have already sent a runner to fetch him. Accept our hospitality in the interim."

Sos got up to leave. "One thing," he said, remembering. "Who is this man?"

"His name is Bog. Bog the club."

Trust wily Tor to think of that! The one warrior not even Sol had been able to defeat.

It was three days before Bog showed up, as big and happy as ever. He had not changed a bit in two years. Sos wanted to rush out and shake the giant's hand and hear him exclaim "Okay!" again, but he could not; he was a nameless stranger now and would have to meet and overcome the man anonymously.

This selection made clear why Tor had arranged the terms as they were. Bog was entirely indifferent to power in the tribal sense. He fought for the sheer joy of action and made no claims upon the vanquished. The messenger had only to whisper "Good fight!" and Bog was on his way.

And Tor had chosen well in another respect, for Bog was the only man Sos knew of who shared virtual physical invulnerability. Others had tried to prevail over the nameless one by skill and had only been vanquished. Bog employed no skill, just inexhaustible power.

The day was waning, and Tor prevailed upon Bog to postpone the battle until morning. "Tough man, long fight," he explained. "Need all day."

Bog's grin widened. "Okay!"

Sos watched the huge man put away food for three and lick his lips in anticipation as several lovely girls clustered solicitously around him and touched the bracelet upon his wrist. Sos felt nostalgia. Here was a man who had an absolute formula for perpetual joy: enormous power, driving appetites and no concern for the future. What a pleasure it would be to travel with him again and bask in the reflected light of his happiness! The reality might have been troubling for others, but never for Bog.

Yet it was to preserve the goodness in the system that he fought now. By defeating Bog he would guarantee that there would always be free warriors for such as Bog to fight. The empire would never swallow them all.

They waited only long enough for the sun to rise to a reasonable height before approaching the circle in the morning. The men of the camp were packed so tightly Tor had to clear a path to the arena. Everyone knew what the stakes were, except possibly Bog himself, who didn't care; but the primary interest was in the combat itself. Only twice, legend said, had Bog been stopped—once by the onset of night and once by a fluke loss of his weapon. No one had ever actually defeated him.

It was also said, however, that he never entered the circle against the net or other unfamiliar weapon.

Bog jumped in, already swinging his club enthusiastically, while Sos remained outside the ring and stripped to his trunks. He folded the long tunic carefully and stood up straight. The two men looked at each other while the audience studied them.

"They're the same size!" a man exclaimed, awed.

Sos started. He, the same size as the giant? Impossible!

Nonetheless, fact. Bog was taller and broader across the shoulders, but Sos was now more solidly constructed. The doctors had given him injections, in the underworld operatory, to stimulate muscular development, and the inserted protective materials added to his mass. He was larger than he had been, and none of the added mass was fat. He probably weighed almost twice what he had when he first set out in search of adventure.

Each man had enormously over-muscled shoulders and arms and a neck sheathed in scars; but where Bog slimmed down to small hips and comparatively puny legs, Sos had a midriff bulging with protective muscles and thighs so thick he found it awkward to run.

Now he carried no weapon: he *was* a weapon.

He stepped into the circle.

Bog proceeded as usual, swinging with indifferent aim at head and body. Sos ducked and took other evasive action. He had stood still to accept the blows of the staff, as a matter of demonstration, but the club was a different matter. A solid hit on the head by such as Bog could knock him senseless. The metal in his skull would not dent, but the brain within would smash itself against the barrier like so much jelly. The reinforced bones of arms and legs would not break, but even the toughened gristle and muscle would suffer if pinched between that

bone and the full force of the club. Bog could hurt him.

Sos avoided the moving club and shot an arm up behind Bog's hand to block the return swing. He leaped inside and drove the other fist into Bog's stomach so hard the man was pushed backward. It was the rock-cracking blow.

Bog shifted hands and brought the weapon savagely down to smash Sos's hip. He stepped back to regain balance and continued the attack. He hadn't noticed the blow.

Sos circled again, exercising the bruised hip and marveling. The man was not exactly flabby in the stomach; that blow could have ruptured the intestines of an ordinary warrior. The way he had shifted grips on his club showed that there was more finesse to his attack than men had given him credit for. As a matter of fact, Bog's swings were not wild at all, now. They shifted angles regularly and the arcs were not wide. There was no time for a sword to cut in between them, or a staff, and lesser weapons would have no chance at all. Bog had an excellent all-purpose defense concealed within his showy offense.

Strange that he had never noticed this before. Was Bog's manifest stupidity an act? Had Sos, who should certainly have known better, assumed that a man as big and strong as Bog must be lacking in mental qualities? Or was Bog a natural fighter, like Sol, who did what he did unconsciously and who won because his instincts were good?

Still, there would be weak points. There had to be. Sos kicked at an exposed knee, hardly having time to set up for the proper angle for dislocation—and had his own leg clipped by a seemingly

accidental descent of the club. He parried the club arm again, leading it out of the way, and leaped to embrace Bog in a bear-hug, catching his two hands together behind the man's back. Bog held his breath and raised the club high in the air and brought it down. Sos let go and shoved him away barely in time to avoid a head blow that would have finished the fight.

Yes, Bog knew how to defend himself.

Next time, Sos blocked the arm and caught it in both hands to apply the breaking pressure. It was no use; Bog tensed his muscles and was too strong. Bog flipped the club to the alternate hand again and blasted away at Sos's back, forcing another hasty retreat. Sos tried once more, pounding his reinforced knuckles into the arm just above the elbow, digging for nerves, but had to let go; the club was too dangerous to ignore. He could do a certain amount of weakening damage to Bog's arms that would, in time, incapacitate the man, but in the meantime he would be subjected to a similar amount of battery by the club, which would hardly leave him in fit condition to fight again soon.

It was apparent that simple measures would not do the job. While consciousness remained, Bog would keep fighting—and he was so constructed that he could not be knocked out easily. A stranglehold from behind? Bog's club could whip over the back or around the side to pulverize the opponent—long before consciousness departed—and how could a forearm do what the rope could not? A hammer-blow to the base of the skull? It was as likely to kill the man as to slow him down, Bog being what he was.

But he was vulnerable. The kick to the crotch, the stiffened finger to the eyeball . . . any rapid blow to a surface organ would surely bring him down.

Sos continued to dodge and parry, forearm against forearm. Should he do it? Did any need justify the deliberate and permanent maiming of a friend?

He didn't argue it. He simply decided to fight as he had to: fairly.

Just as the club would knock him out once it connected, so one of his own blows or grips would bring down Bog, when properly executed. Since Bog didn't know the meaning of defeat, and would never give in to numbing blows or simple pain, there was no point in such tactics. He would have to end the contest swiftly and decisively—which meant accepting at least one full smash from the club as he set up his position. It was a necessary risk.

Sos timed the next pass, spun away from it, ducked his head and thrust out in the high stamping kick aimed for Bog's chin. The club caught him at the thigh, stunning the muscle and knocking him sidewise, but his heel landed.

Too high. It caught Bog's forehead and snapped his head back with force abetted by the impact of the club upon his leg. A much more dangerous blow than the one intended.

Sos dropped to the ground, rolled over to get his good leg under him, and leaped up again, ready to follow up with a sustained knuckle-beat to the back of the neck. Bog could not swing effectively so long as he was pinned to the ground, and even he could not withstand more than a few seconds of—

Sos halted. Suddenly he knew what had happened. The slight misplacement of the kick, providing added leverage against the head; the forward thrust of Bog's large body as he swung; the feedback effect of the club blow upon the leg; the very musculature constricting the clubber's neck—these things had combined to make the very special connection Sos had sought to avoid.

Bog's neck was broken.

He was not dead—but the damage was irreparable, here. If he survived, it would be as a paralytic. Bog would never fight again.

Sos looked up, becoming aware of the audience he had completely forgotten, and met Tor's eyes. Tor nodded gravely.

Sos picked up Bog's club and smashed it with all his force against the staring head.

20

"C OME WITH ME," SAV SAID. Sos followed him into the forest, paying no attention to the direction. He felt as he had when Stupid perished in the snow. Here was a great, perhaps slow-witted but happy fellow—abruptly dead in a manner no one had wanted or expected, least of all Sos himself. Sos had liked the hearty clubber; he had fought by his side. By the definition of the circle, Bog had been his friend.

There were many ways he could have killed the man, had that been his intent, or maimed him, despite his power. Sos's efforts to avoid doing any real damage had been largely responsible for the prolongation of the encounter—yet had led to nothing. Perhaps there had been no way to defeat Bog without killing him.

Perhaps in time Sos could convince himself of that, anyway.

At least he had seen to it that the man died as he might have wished: by a swift blow from the club. Small comfort.

Sav stopped and gestured. They were in a forest glade, a circular mound with a small, crude pyramid of stones at the apex. It was one of the places of burial and worship maintained by volunteer tribesmen who did not choose to turn over the bodies of their friends to the crazies for cremation.

"In the underworld—could they have saved him?" Sav inquired.

"I think so."

"But if you tried to take him there—"

"They would have blasted us both with the flamethrower before we got within hailing distance of the entrance. I am forbidden ever to return."

"Then, this is best," Sav said.

They stood looking at the mound, knowing that Bog would soon lie within it.

"Sol comes to these churches every few days, alone," Sav said. "I thought you'd like to know."

Then it seemed that no time passed, but it had been a month of travel and healing, and he was standing beside another timeless mound and Sol was coming to pray.

Sol knelt at the foot of the pyramid and raised his eyes to it. Sos dropped to his own knees beside him. They stayed there in silence for some time.

"I had a friend," Sos said at last. "I had to meet him in the circle, though I would not have chosen it. Now he is buried here."

"I, too," Sol said. "He went to the mountain."

"Now I must challenge for an empire I do not want, and perhaps kill again, when all that I desire is friendship."

"I prayed here all day for friendship," Sol said, speaking of all the mounds in the world as one, and all times as one, as Sos had done. "When I returned to my camp I thought my prayer was answered—but he required what I could not give." He paused. "I would give my empire to have that friend again."

"Why can't we two walk away from here, never to enter the circle again?"

"I would take only my daughter." He looked at Sos, for the first time since staff and rope had parted, and if he recognized him as anything more than the heralded nameless challenger, or found this unheralded mode of contact strange, he did not say. "I would give you her mother, since your bracelet is dead."

"I would accept her, in the name of friendship."

"In the name of friendship."

They stood up and shook hands. It was as close as they could come to acknowledging recognition.

The camp was monstrous. Five of the remaining tribes had migrated to rejoin their master, anticipating the arrival of the challenger. Two thousand men spread across plain and forest with their families, sleeping in communal tents and eating at communal hearths. Literate men supervised distribution of supplies and gave daily instruction in reading and figuring to groups of apprentices. Parties trekked into the mountains, digging for the ore that the books said was there, while others cultivated the ground to grow the nutritive plants that other books said could be

raised. Women practiced weaving and knitting in groups, and one party had a crude native loom. The empire was now too large to feed itself from the isolated cabins of a single area, too independent to depend upon any external source for clothing or weapons.

"This is Sola," Sol said, introducing the elegant, sultry high lady. He spoke to her: "I would give you to the nameless one. He is a powerful warrior, though he carries no weapon."

"As you wish," she said indifferently. She glanced at Sos, and through him. "Where is his bracelet? What should I call myself?"

"Keep the clasp I gave you. I will find another."

"Keep the name you bear, I have none better."

"You're crazy," she said, addressing both.

"This is Soli," Sol said as the little girl entered the compartment. He picked her up and held her at head height. She grasped a tiny staff and waved it dangerously.

"I'm a Amazon!" she said, poking the stick at Sos. "I'm fighting in circle."

They moved on to the place where the chieftains gathered: Sav and Tyl together, Tor and Tun, and Neq and three others Sos did not recognize in another group. They spread out to form a standing circle as Sol and Sos approached.

"We have reached a tentative agreement on terms," Sav said. "Subject to approval by the two masters, of course."

"The terms are these," Sol said, not giving him a chance to continue. "The empire will be disbanded. Each of you will command the tribe you now govern in our names, and Tor his old tribe, but you will never meet each other in the circle."

They stared at him uncomprehendingly. "You fought already?" Tun inquired.

"I have quit the circle."

"Then we must serve the nameless one."

"I have quit the circle too," Sos said.

"But the empire will fall apart without one of you as master. No one else is strong enough!"

Sol turned his back on them. "It is done," he said. "Let's take our things and go."

"Wait a minute!" Tyl exclaimed, running stiff-legged after them. "You owe us an explanation."

Sol shrugged, offering none. Sos turned about and spoke. "Four years ago you all served small tribes or traveled alone. You slept in cabins or in private tents, and you did not need anything that was not provided. You were free to go and to live as you chose.

"Now you travel in large tribes and you fight for other men when they tell you to. You till the land, working as the crazies do, because your numbers are too great for the resources of any one area. You mine for metals, because you no longer trust the crazies to do it for you, though they have never broken trust. You study from books, because you want the things civilization can offer. But this is not the way it should be. We know what civilization leads to. It brings destruction of all the values of the circle. It brings competition for material things you do not need. Before long you will overpopulate the Earth and become a scourge upon it, like shrews who have overrun their feeding grounds.

"The records show that the end result of empire is—the Blast."

But he hadn't said it well.

All but Sav peered incredulously at him. "You claim," Tor said slowly, "that unless we remain primitive nomads, dependent upon the crazies, ignorant of finer things, there will be a second Blast?"

"In time, yes. That is what happened before. It is our duty to see that it never happens again."

"And you believe that the answer is to keep things as they are, disorganized?"

"Yes."

"So more men like Bog can die in the circle?"

Sos stood as if stricken. Was he on the right side, after all?

"Better that, than that we all die in the Blast," Sol put in surprisingly. "There are not enough of us, now, to recover again."

Unwittingly, he had undercut Sos's argument, since overpopulation was the problem of empire.

Neq turned on Sol. "Yet you preserve the circle by deserting it!"

Sav, who understood both sides, finally spoke. "Sometimes you have to give up something you love, something you value, so as not to destroy it. I'd call that sensible enough."

"I'd call it cowardice!" Tyl said.

Both Sol and Sos jumped toward him angrily.

Tyl stood firm. "Each of you defeated me in the circle. I will serve either. But if you fear to face each other for supremacy, I must call you what you are."

"You have no right to build an empire and throw it away like that," Tor said. "Leadership means responsibility."

"Where did you learn all this 'history'?" Neq demanded. "I don't believe it."

"We're just beginning to cooperate like men, instead of playing like children," Tun said.

Sol looked at Sos. "They have no power over us. Let them talk."

Sos stood indecisively. What these suddenly assertive men were saying made distressing sense. How could he be sure that what the master of the underworld had told him was true? There were so many obvious advantages of civilization—and it had taken thousands of years for the Blast to come, before. Had it really been the fault of civilization, or had there been factors he didn't know about? Factors that might no longer exist. . . .

Little Soli appeared and ran toward Sol. "Are you going to fight now, Daddy?"

Tyl stepped ahead of him and managed to intercept her, squatting with difficulty since his knees were still healing. "Soli, what would you do if your daddy decided not to fight?"

She presented him with the round-eyed stare. "Not fight?"

No one else spoke.

"If he said he wouldn't go in the circle any more," Tyl prompted her. "If he went away and never fought again."

Soil burst out crying.

Tyl let her go. She ran to Sol. "You go in the circle, Daddy!" she exclaimed. "Show him!"

It had happened again. Sol faced him, defeated. "I must fight for my daughter."

Sos struggled with himself, but knew that the peaceful settlement had flown. He saw, in a terrible revelation, that this,

not name, woman or empire, had been the root of each of their encounters: the child. The child called Soli had been there throughout; the circle had determined which man would claim the name and privilege of fatherhood.

Sol could not back down, and neither could Sos. Bob, of the underworld, had made clear what would happen if Sos allowed the empire to stand.

"Tomorrow, then," Sos said, also defeated.

"Tomorrow—friend."

"And the winner rules the empire—all of it!" Tyl shouted, and the others agreed.

Why did their smiles look lupine?

They ate together, the two masters with Sola and Soli. "You will take care of my daughter," Sol said. He did not need to define the circumstance further.

Sos only nodded.

Sola was more direct. "Do you want me tonight?"

Was this the woman he had longed for? Sos studied her, noting the voluptuous figure, the lovely features. She did not recognize him, he was certain—yet she had accepted an insulting alliance with complacency.

"She—loved another," Sol said. "Now nothing matters to her, except power. It is not her fault."

"I still love him," she said. "If his body is dead, his memory is not. My own body does not matter."

Sos continued to look at her—but the image he saw was of little Sosa of the underworld, the girl who wore his bracelet. The girl Bob had threatened to send in his place, should Sos refuse to undertake the mission . . . to work her way into Sol's camp as anybody's woman and to stab Sol with a poisoned dart and then herself, leaving the master of empire dead and disgraced. The girl who would *still* be sent, if Sos failed.

At first it had been Sol's fate that had concerned him, though Bob never suspected this. Only by agreeing to the mission could Sos arrange to turn aside its treachery. But as the time of training passed, Sosa's own peril had become as important. If he betrayed the underworld now, she would pay the penalty.

Sola and Sosa: the two had never met, yet they controlled his destiny. He had to act to protect them both—and he dared tell neither why.

"In the name of friendship, take her!" Sol exclaimed. "I have nothing left to offer."

"In the name of friendship," Sos whispered. He was sickened by the whole affair, so riddled with sacrifice and dishonor. He knew that the man Sola embraced in her mind would be the one who had gone to the mountain. She might never know the truth.

And the woman *he* embraced would be Sosa. *She* would never know, either. He had not realized until he left her that he loved her more.

At noon the next day they met at the circle. Sos wished there were some way he could lose, but he knew at the same moment that this was no solution. Sol's victory would mean his death; the underworld had pronounced it.

Twice he had met Sol in battle, striving to win and failing. This time he would strive in his heart to lose, but had to win. Better the humiliation of one, than the death of two.

Sol had chosen the daggers. His handsome body glistened in the sunlight—but Sos imagined with sadness the way that body would look after the terrible hands of the nameless one closed upon it. He looked for some pretext to delay the onset, but found none. The watchers were massed and waiting, and the commitment had been made. The masters had to meet, and there was no friendship in the circle. Sos would spare his friend if he were able—but he had to win.

They entered the circle together and faced each other for a moment, each respecting the other's capabilities. Perhaps each still hoped for some way to stop it, even now. There was no way. It had been unrealistic to imagine that this final encounter could be reneged. They were the masters: no longer, paradoxically, their own masters.

Sos made the first move. He jumped close and drove a sledgehammer fist at Sol's stomach—and caught his balance as the effort came to nothing. Sol had stepped aside, as he had to, moving more swiftly than seemed possible, as he always did—and a shallow slash ran the length of the challenger's forearm. The fist had missed, the knife had not wounded seriously, and the first testing of skill had been accomplished.

Sos had known better than to follow up with a second blow in the moment Sol appeared to be off-balance. Sol was never caught unaware. Sol had refrained from committing the other knife, knowing that the seeming ponderosity of Sos's hands was illusory. Tactics and strategy at this level of skill looked crude only because so many simple ploys were useless or suicidal; finesse seemed like bluff only to the uninitiate.

They circled each other, watching the placements of feet and balance of torso rather than face or hands. The expression in a face could lie, but not the attitude of the body; the motion of a hand could switch abruptly, but not that of a foot. No major commitment could be made without preparation and reaction. Thus Sol seemed to hold the twin blades lightly while Sos hardly glanced at them.

Sol moved, sweeping both points in toward the body, one high, the other low. Sos's hands were there, closing about the two wrists as the knives were balked by protected shoulder and belly, and Sol pinioned. He applied pressure slowly, knowing that the real ploy had not yet been executed.

Sol was strong, but he could not hope to compete with his opponent's power. Gradually his arms bent down as the vice-like grip intensified, and the fingers on the knives loosened. Then Sol flexed both wrists—and they spun about within the grip! No wonder his body shone: he had greased it.

Now the daggers took on life of their own, flipping over together to center on the imprisoning manacles. The points dug in, braced against clamped hands, feeling for the vulnerable tendons, and they were feather-sharp.

Sos had to let go. His hardened skin could deflect lightning slashes, but not the anchored probing he was exposed to here. He released one wrist only, yanking tremendously at the other trying to break it while his foot lashed against the man's inner thigh. But Sol's free blade whipped across unerringly, to bury itself in the flesh of Sos's other forearm, and it was not the thigh but the hard bone of hip that met the moving foot. It was far more dangerous to break with Sol than to close with him.

They parted, the one with white marks showing the crushing pressure exerted against him, the other with spot punctures and streaming blood from one arm. The second testing had passed. It was known that if the nameless one could catch the daggers, he could not hold them, and the experienced witnesses nodded gravely. The one was stronger, the other faster, and the advantage of the moment lay with Sol.

The battle continued. Bruises appeared upon Sol's body, and countless cuts blossomed on Sos's, but neither scored definitely. It had become a contest of attrition.

This could go on for a long time, and no one wanted that. A definite decision was required, not a suspect draw. One master had to prevail or the other. By a certain unvoiced mutual consent they cut short the careful sparring and played for the ultimate stakes.

Sol dived, in a motion similar to the one Sos had used against him during their first encounter, going not for the almost invulnerable torso, but the surface muscles and tendons of the legs. Sol's success would cripple Sos, and put him at a fatal disadvantage. He leaped aside, but the two blades followed as Sol twisted like a serpent. He was on his back now, feet in the air, ready to smite the attacker. He had been so adept at nullifying prior attacks that Sos was sure the man was at least partially familiar with weaponless techniques. This might also explain Sol's phenomenal success as a warrior. The only real advantage Sos had was brute strength.

He used it. He hunched his shoulders and fell upon Sol, pinning him by the weight of his body and closing both hands about his throat. Sol's two knives came up, their motion restricted but not blocked, and stabbed into the gristle on either side of Sos's own neck. The force of each blow was not great, since the position was quite awkward, but the blades drove again and again into the widening wounds. The neck was the best protected part of his body, but it could not sustain this attack for long.

Sos lifted himself and hurled the lighter man from side to side, never relinquishing the cruel constriction, but his position, too, was improper for full effect. Then, as his head took fire with the exposure of vital nerves, he knew that he was losing this phase; the blades would bring him down before Sol finally relinquished that tenacious consciousness.

It would not be possible to finish it gently.

He broke, catching Sol's hair to hold his head down, and hammered his horny knuckle into the exposed windpipe.

Sol could not breathe and was in excruciating pain. His throat had been crushed. Still the awful daggers searched for Sos's face, seeking, if not victory, mutual defeat. It was not in Sol to lose in the circle.

Sos used his strength once more. He caught one blade in his hand, knowing that the edge could not slip free from his flesh. With the other hand he grabbed again for the hair. He stood up, carrying Sol's body with him. He whirled about—and flung his friend out of the circle.

As quickly as he had possession of the circle, he abdicated it, diving after his fallen antagonist. Sol lay on the ground, eyes bulging, hands clasping futilely at his throat. Sos ripped them away and dug his fingers into the sides of the neck,

massaging it roughly. His own blood dripped upon Sol's chest as he squatted above him.

"It's over!" someone screamed. "You're out of the circle! Stop!"

Sos did not stop. He picked one dagger from the ground and cut into the base of Sol's throat, using the knowledge his training in destruction had provided.

A body fell upon him, but he was braced against it. He lifted one great arm and flung the person away without looking. He widened the incision until a small hole opened in Sol's trachea; then he put his mouth to the wound.

More men fell upon him, yanking at his arms and legs, but he clung fast. Air rushed into the unconscious man's lungs as Sos exhaled, and his friend was breathing again, precariously.

"Sav! It's me, Sav," a voice bellowed in his ear, "Red River! Let go! I'll take over!"

Only then did Sos lift bloodflecked lips and surrender to unconsciousness.

He woke to pain shooting along his neck. His hand found bandages there. Sola leaned over him, soft of expression, and mopped the streaming sweat from his face with a cool sponge. "I know you," she murmured as she saw his eyes open. "I'll never leave you—nameless one."

Sos tried to speak, but not even the croak came out. "Yes, you saved him," she said. "Again. He can't talk any more, but he's in better shape than you are. Even though you won." She leaned down to kiss him lightly. "It was brave of you to rescue him like that—but nothing is changed."

Sos sat up. His neck exploded into agony as he put stress upon it, and he could not turn his head, but he kept on grimly. He was in the main tent, in what was evidently Sola's compartment. He looked about by swiveling his body. No one else was present.

Sola took his arm gently. "I'll wake you before he goes. I promise. Now lie down before you kill yourself—again."

Everything seemed to be repeating. She had cared for him like this once long ago, and he had fallen in love with her. When he needed help, she was—

Then it was another day. "It's time," she said, waking him with a kiss. She had donned her most elegant clothing and was as beautiful as he had ever seen her. It had been premature to discount his love for her; it had not died.

Sol was standing outside with his daughter, a bandage on his throat and discoloration remaining on his body, but otherwise fit and strong. He smiled when he saw Sos and came over to shake hands. No words were necessary. Then he placed Soli's little hand in Sos's and turned away.

The men of the camp stood in silence as Sol walked past them, away from the tent. He wore a pack but carried no weapon.

"Daddy!" Soli cried, wrenching away from Sos and running after him.

Sav jumped out and caught her. "He goes to the mountain," he explained gently. "You must stay with your mother and your new father."

Soli struggled free again and caught up to Sol. "Daddy!" Sol turned, kneeled, kissed her and turned her to face the way she had come. He stood up quickly and resumed his walk. Sos remembered the time he had tried to send Stupid down the mountain.

"Daddy!" she cried once more, refusing to leave him. "I go with you!" Then, to show she understood: "I die with you."

Sol turned again and looked beseechingly at the assembled men.

No one moved.

Finally he picked Soli up and walked out of the camp.

Sola put her face to Sos's shoulder and sobbed silently, refusing to go after her daughter. "She belongs to him," she said through her tears. "She always did."

As he watched the lonely figures depart, Sos saw what was in store for them. Sol would ascend the mountain, carrying the little girl. He would not be daunted by the snow or the death that waited him. He would drive on until overwhelmed by the cold, and fall at last with his face toward the top, shielding his daughter's body with his own until the end.

Sos knew what would happen then, and who would be waiting to adopt a gallant husband and a darling daughter. There would be the chase in the recreation room, perhaps, and special exercise for Soli. It had to be, for Sosa would recognize the child. The child she had longed to bear herself.

Take her! he thought. Take her—in the name of love.

While Sos remained to be the architect of the empire's quiet destruction, never certain whether he was doing the right thing. He had built it in the name of another man; now he would bring it down at the behest of a selfish power clique whose purpose was to prevent civilization from arising on the surface. To prevent *power* from arising.

Sos had always been directed in key decisions by the action of other men, just as his romancing had been directed by those women who reached for it. Sol had given him his name and first mission; Dr. Jones had given him his weapon; Sol had sent him to the mountain and Bob had sent him back. Sol's lieutenants had forced the mastership upon him, not realizing that he was the enemy of the empire.

Would the time ever come when he made his own decisions? The threat that had existed against Sol now applied against Sos: if he did not dismantle the empire, someone would come for him, someone he would have no way to recognize or guard against, and hostages would die. Three of them, one a child . . .

He looked at Sola, lovely in her sorrow, and knew that the woman he loved more would belong to Sol. Nothing had changed. Dear little Sosa—

Sos faced the men of his empire, thousands strong. They thought him master now—but was he the hero, or the villain?

ABOUT THE AUTHOR

New York Times bestseller Piers Anthony (1934–) is one of the most prominent and prolific science fiction and fantasy authors of all time. In addition to more than a hundred unrelated novels (including one title for each letter of the alphabet, from *Anthonology* to *Zombie Lover*), his wildly popular Xanth series is currently 34 books long and growing, its unique brand of lighthearted fantasy remaining a high-profile staple of the genre since its inception in 1977.

Collect all of these exciting Planet Stories adventures!

STEPPE
BY PIERS ANTHONY
INTRODUCTION BY CHRIS ROBERSON

After facing a brutal death at the hands of enemy tribesmen upon the Eurasian steppe, the ninth-century warrior-chieftain Alp awakes fifteen hundred years in the future only to find himself a pawn in a ruthless game that spans the stars.

ISBN: 978-1-60125-182-4

BEFORE THEY WERE GIANTS
EDITED BY JAMES L. SUTTER

See where it all began! In this exclusive collection, fifteen of the greatest living science fiction and fantasy authors, from Piers Anthony and Ben Bova to William Gibson and China Miéville, present and critique their first published SF stories, offering brand new interviews filled with anecdotes and advice. A must-have for any serious fan, scholar, or aspiring writer.

ISBN: 978-1-60125-266-1

THE SECRET OF SINHARAT
BY LEIGH BRACKETT
INTRODUCTION BY MICHAEL MOORCOCK

In the Martian Drylands, a criminal conspiracy leads wild man Eric John Stark to a secret that could shake the Red Planet to its core. In a bonus novel, *People of the Talisman*, Stark ventures to the polar ice cap of Mars to return a stolen talisman to an oppressed people.

ISBN: 978-1-60125-047-6

THE GINGER STAR
BY LEIGH BRACKETT
INTRODUCTION BY BEN BOVA

Eric John Stark journeys to the dying world of Skaith in search of his kidnapped foster father, only to find himself the subject of a revolutionary prophecy. In completing his mission, will he be forced to fulfill the prophecy as well?

ISBN: 978-1-60125-084-1

THE HOUNDS OF SKAITH
BY LEIGH BRACKETT
INTRODUCTION BY F. PAUL WILSON

Eric John Stark has destroyed the Citadel of the Lords Protector, but the war for Skaith's freedom is just beginning. Together with his foster father Simon Ashton, Stark will have to unite some of the strangest and most bloodthirsty peoples the galaxy has ever seen if he ever wants to return home.

ISBN: 978-1-60125-135-0

THE REAVERS OF SKAITH
BY LEIGH BRACKETT
INTRODUCTION BY GEORGE LUCAS

Betrayed and left to die on a savage planet, Eric John Stark and his foster father Simon Ashton must ally with cannibals and feral warriors to topple an empire and bring an enslaved civilization to the stars. But in fulfilling the prophecy, will Stark sacrifice that which he values most?

ISBN: 978-1-60125-084-1

Black God's Kiss
by C. L. Moore
Introduction by Suzy McKee Charnas

The first female sword and sorcery protagonist takes up her greatsword and challenges dark gods and monsters in the groundbreaking stories that made her famous and inspired a generation of female authors. Of particular interest to fans of Robert E. Howard and H. P. Lovecraft.

ISBN: 978-1-60125-045-2

The Swordsman of Mars
by Otis Adelbert Kline
Introduction by Michael Moorcock

Harry Thorne, outcast scion of a wealthy East Coast family, swaps bodies with a Martian in order to hunt down another Earthman before he corrupts an empire. Trapped between two beautiful women, will Harry end up a slave, or rise up and claim his destiny as a swordsman of Mars?

ISBN: 978-1-60125-105-3

Robots Have No Tails
by Henry Kuttner
Introduction by F. Paul Wilson

Heckled by an uncooperative robot, a binge-drinking inventor must solve the mystery of his own machines before his dodgy financing and reckless lifestyle get the better of him. Collects all five classic "Gallegher" stories!

ISBN: 978-1-60125-153-4

Elak of Atlantis
by Henry Kuttner
Introduction by Joe R. Lansdale

A dashing swordsman with a mysterious past battles his way across ancient Atlantis in the stories that helped found the sword and sorcery genre. Also includes two rare tales featuring Prince Raynor of Imperial Gobi!

ISBN: 978-1-60125-046-9

The Dark World
by Henry Kuttner
Introduction by Piers Anthony

Sucked through a portal into an alternate dimension, Edward Bond finds himself trapped in the body of the evil wizard Ganelon. Will Bond-as-Ganelon free the Dark World from its oppressors—or take on the mantle of its greatest villain?

ISBN: 978-1-60125-136-7

The Outlaws of Mars
by Otis Adelbert Kline
Introduction by Joe R. Lansdale

Transported through space by powers beyond his understanding, Earthman Jerry Morgan lands on the Red Planet only to find himself sentenced to death for a crime he didn't commit. Hunted by both sides of a vicious civil war and spurned by the beautiful princess he loves, Jerry soon finds he must lead a revolution to dethrone his Martian overlords—or die trying!

ISBN: 978-1-60125-151-0

INFERNAL SORCERESS
BY GARY GYGAX
INTRODUCTION BY ERIK MONA

When the shadowy Ferret and the broad-shouldered mercenary Raker are framed for the one crime they *didn't* commit, the scoundrels are faced with a choice: bring the true culprits to justice, or dance a gallows jig. Can even this canny, ruthless duo prevail against the beautiful witch that plots their downfall?

ISBN: 978-1-60125-117-6

THE ANUBIS MURDERS
BY GARY GYGAX
INTRODUCTION BY ERIK MONA

Someone is murdering the world's most powerful sorcerers, and the trail of blood leads straight to Anubis, the solemn god known by most as the Master of Jackals. Can Magister Setne Inhetep, personal philosopher-wizard to the Pharaoh, reach the distant kingdom of Avillonia and put an end to the Anubis Murders, or will he be claimed as the latest victim?

ISBN: 978-1-60125-042-1

THE SAMARKAND SOLUTION
BY GARY GYGAX
INTRODUCTION BY ED GREENWOOD

Death has come to the Ægyptian city of On, and only Magister Setne Inhetep, wizard-priest and detective in the service of Pharaoh, has a chance of solving the mystery in time to stop a bloody rebellion.

ISBN: 978-1-60125-083-4

DEATH IN DELHI
BY GARY GYGAX
INTRODUCTION BY JAMES LOWDER

Magister Setne Inhetep must travel to the land of the Peacock Throne to recover the stolen Crown Jewels of the Maharajah. There he will face pirates and assassins, death cultists and black magic—and if he is not careful, meet his fate at the many hands of Kali, Goddess of Death . . .

ISBN: 978-1-60125-137-4

WORLDS OF THEIR OWN
EDITED BY JAMES LOWDER

From R. A. Salvatore and Ed Greenwood to Michael A. Stackpole and Elaine Cunningham, shared world books have launched the careers of some of SF's largest names. Yet what happens when these authors write tales in worlds entirely of their own devising? Contains 18 stories by the genre's biggest authors.

ISBN: 978-1-60125-118-3

THE SHIP OF ISHTAR
BY A. MERRITT
INTRODUCTION BY TIM POWERS

When amateur archaeologist John Kenton breaks open a strange stone block from ancient Babylon, he finds himself hurled through time and space onto the deck of a golden ship sailing the seas of another dimension—caught between the goddess Ishtar and the pale warriors of the Black God.

ISBN: 978-1-60125-118-3

Read HOW THESE MEN GOT BETTER BOOKS
THEN FIND OUT WHAT PLANET STORIES OFFERS YOU *Subscribe!*

PLANET STORIES SHIPS A BEAUTIFUL NEW SCIENCE FICTION OR FANTASY BOOK DIRECT TO MY DOOR EVERY 60 DAYS AT 30% OFF THE COVER PRICE. ALL I NEED TO DO IS SIT BACK AND READ!

ALEXANDER BLADE,
NEW YORK CITY, NEW YORK.

WITH THE GREAT CLASSIC REPRINTS OFFERED BY PLANET STORIES, I'VE LEARNED MORE ABOUT THE HISTORY OF SCIENCE FICTION AND FANTASY THAN EVER BEFORE. MY FRIENDS THINK I'M AN EXPERT!

S.M. TENNESHAW,
BOSTON, MASS.

THESE BOOKS ARE THE PERFECT COMPANIONS WHEN I'M JET-SETTING ACROSS THE WORLD. ALL MY PASSENGERS ENVY THE TOP-QUALITY FICTION PLANET STORIES PROVIDES.

CAPTAIN CURTIS NEWTON,
PATRIOT AIRWAYS,
YORBA LINDA, CA.

I'M A TABLETOP GAMER, AND PLANET STORIES GIVES ME AN EXCITING LOOK AT THE ADVENTURE FICTION THAT INSPIRED MY FAVORITE HOBBY. YOU SHOULD SEE HOW I USE THE MONSTERS IN MY CAMPAIGN!

DICK AWLINSON,
LAKE GENEVA, WIS.

WITH MY PLANET STORIES SUBSCRIPTION, I NEED NEVER WORRY ABOUT MISSING A SINGLE VOLUME. I CAN CHOOSE THE DELIVERY METHOD THAT WORKS BEST FOR ME, AND THE SUBSCRIPTION LASTS UNTIL I DECIDE TO CANCEL.

N.W. SMITH,
SCHENECTADY, NEW YORK.

I CAN COMBINE MY PLANET STORIES BOOKS WITH OTHER SUBSCRIPTIONS FROM PAIZO.COM, SAVING MONEY ON SHIPPING AND HANDLING CHARGES!

MATTHEW CARSE,
KAHORA, MARS

FINE BOOKS FOR FINE MINDS
SUBSCRIBE TODAY

Explore fantastic worlds of high adventure with a genuine Planet Stories subscription that delivers the excitement of classic fantasy and science fiction right to your mailbox! Best of all, you'll receive your bi-monthly Planet Stories volumes at a substantial 30% discount off the cover price, and you can choose the shipping method that works best for you (including bundling the books with your other Paizo subscriptions)!

Only the Finest SF Books
The Best of Yesterday and Today!

Personally selected by publisher Erik Mona and Paizo's award-winning editorial staff, each Planet Stories volume has been chosen with the interests of fantasy and science fiction enthusiasts and gamers in mind. Timeless classics from authors like Robert E. Howard (Conan the Barbarian), Michael Moorcock (Elric), and Leigh Brackett (*The Empire Strikes Back*) will add an edge to your personal library, providing a better understanding of the genre with classic stories that easily stand the test of time.

Each Planet Stories edition is a Paizo exclusive—you cannot get these titles from any other publisher. Many of the tales in our line first appeared in the "pulp era" of the early 20th Century that

produced authors like H. P. Lovecraft, Edgar Rice Burroughs, Fritz Leiber, and Robert E. Howard, and have been out of print for decades. Others are available only in rare limited editions or moldering pulp magazines worth hundreds of dollars.

Why Spend $20, $50, or even $100 to Read a Story?
Smart Readers Make Smart Subscribers

Sign up for an ongoing Planet Stories subscription to make sure that you don't miss a single volume! Subscriptions are fixed at a 30% discount off each volume's cover price, plus shipping. Your ongoing Planet Stories subscription will get you every new book as it's released, automatically continuing roughly every 60 days until you choose to cancel your subscription. After your

BEST OF ALL, AS A SUBSCRIBER, I ALSO RECEIVE A 15% DISCOUNT ON THE DOZENS OF BOOKS ALREADY PUBLISHED IN THE PLANET STORIES LIBRARY!

WILL GARTH,
CHICAGO, ILL.

first subscription volume ships, you'll also receive a 15% discount on the entire Planet Stories library! Instead of paying for your subscription all at once, we'll automatically charge your credit card before we ship a new volume. You only need to sign up once, and never need to worry about renewal notices or missed volumes!

Visit paizo.com/planetstories to subscribe today!

PLANET STORIES AUTHORS

Piers Anthony
Leigh Brackett
Gary Gygax

Robert E. Howard
Otis Adelbert Kline
Henry Kuttner

Michael Moorcock
C. L. Moore

STRANGE ADVENTURES ON OTHER WORLDS

PLANET
stories